MURDER

WAS THE

CASE

BUY

FOR MELODRAMA

MURDER

WAS THE

CASE

KIKI SWINSON

www.melodramapublishing.com

Library of Congress Control Number: 2012934064
ISBN-13: 978-1934157541
ISBN-10: 1934157546
First Edition: September 2012
10 9 8 7 6 5 4 3 2 1

Interior Design: Candace K. Cottrell
Cover Design: Marion Designs
Model: DAWN MONTGOMERY-GREEN

Also By
KIKI SWINSON

FLORIDA BOUND

I was housed in the Chesapeake County Jail for six weeks before my extradition papers were finally processed. CO Dutton told me the U.S. Marshals were scheduled to pick me up in a few days. She'd just clocked in for her shift a few minutes earlier and didn't waste any time coming down to my unit to tell me. She was a sweetheart. From the very first day I'd gotten there, she'd treated me like a human being.

All the other corrections officers treated me like shit. I heard some of them call me a cop killer, but I learned to ignore them. They knew nothing about me. They had no idea what I was really about, so I learned to keep my head up and wait until I was able to clear my name. Most of the female inmates treated me like a celebrity, but a few called me cop killer. That shit didn't faze me one bit as long as they knew not to put their fucking hands on me. I was a small woman in height, but I would've fucked up any bitch in there dumb enough to test me.

There was one cool inmate by the name of Tina Elroy. She was a bunkie. My roommate, if you want to get technical. She was twice my size, but she was pretty. I never asked her age, but she looked to be about thirty-five. She was Caucasian but acted black. Everyone in the jail knew her. It didn't take me long to find out that she was a repeat offender, which was why she was so popular. What kept her in jail was identity theft and check fraud. She couldn't keep her hands out of other people's credit reports to save her life.

I had asked her one time how much she made off stealing other people's personal information, and when she told me that she only got one hundred dollars per victim, I laughed in her face. She looked at me like I was crazy, so I broke it down to her and told her she had been played. I told her that she needed to get her life together, because this jail shit isn't for women.

She told me she had a drug habit, which, to me, explained why she accepted so little for the information she stole and sold. At that moment, I looked at her and thought about how my life could have ended up if I had started using drugs really heavy again. It was bad enough I was in a fucked up situation, but if I had let my coke habit continue, there was no telling how I would have ended up.

From the first day Tina and I started talking, we formed a bond. I didn't have much while I was sitting in that hellhole, but Mario made sure I had the necessities. I shared everything with Tina, and in return, she had my back, just in case any of the bitches in there wanted to put their hands on me. She was my personal bodyguard.

"Lomax, you got mail," CO Dutton yelled from the other side of the metal bars.

I hopped from my bunk and dashed toward her. She held out a manila envelope. I smiled as I took it from her hands.

"Looks like you got yourself a good man." She walked away from the cellblock.

I nodded and remained silent. There were too many hoes lingering around listening, so I made it my business to keep my personal life hush-hush. I climbed back onto my bed and wasted no time pulling the contents of the envelope out.

Tina walked into our cell at the exact same time I revealed the contents of the envelope. She smiled at me when she saw the card. She didn't have to say anything; she knew it came from Mario. She did, however, comment on how pretty it was.

"It is pretty, isn't it?" I looked the card over.

She stood there and watched me as I opened it up and read it. There were only four lines to read, so it didn't take me long to retain every word.

I looked back up from the card and smiled at Tina. "Girl, I don't know what I am going to do with this guy."

"What does it say?"

"He told me he is going to stick by my side through this whole thing, and when it's all over, he wants us to get married."

"Really!"

I nodded.

"So what are you going to do?"

"What do you mean?" I asked her.

"Are you going to marry him?"

I sighed and then I said, "Tina, as much as I want to, I don't think it's gonna happen."

"Why not?"

"You already know what I've got to go up against when I get back to Miami."

"Yeah. And?"

"What if I get railroaded and lose my case? Mario isn't gonna want to marry me if they stick a life sentence on my back."

"I understand what you're saying, but that's not gonna happen."

She patted me on my leg. "You're gonna be fine. Especially with those attorneys you said he hired to work your case. So stop worrying yourself. Everything is going to be all right. Watch."

"I hope you're right." I inserted the card back inside the manila envelope. Afterward, I tucked the envelope under my pillow.

Tina smiled at me. "Just do me a favor when you get out."

"And what's that?"

"Send me a few dollars to put on my commissary, so I can have some money when they send me off to the women's prison in Goochland."

"Don't worry. I gotcha covered."

A few seconds later I slid back off my bunk and exited my cell, leaving Tina standing at the doorway.

"Where you going?" she asked.

"To call my man." I smiled.

"You better hurry up because there's only one phone available."

I raced down to the other end of the cellblock. The chicks on my cellblock were off the chain. They would babysit the pay phones like they gave birth to them. It was really hard to get a phone when they were tied up, so when one came available, you had to grab it up quickly, or you'd be waiting around for hours just to make a fifteen-minute call to your loved ones.

I'd witnessed one woman almost get her head knocked off because she wouldn't get off the phone. It was crazy in there. The women acted like damn fools, and I wasn't trying to get involved with their antics.

After I grabbed a hold of the phone, I dialed Mario's number and waited for the jail phone system to connect the call. It took about forty seconds for it to happen.

When I heard him say, "Hello," I melted on the inside.

It took an additional five seconds for him to wait for the prompt to accept the charges.

"What's up, baby?" he rushed to say.

I smiled. The sound of his voice always made me smile, and I couldn't keep it a secret. "I got your card."

"Did you like it?"

"Oh my God, Mario, it was so beautiful. Thank you so much."

"You're welcome, baby."

"Well, I also called to tell you that I just found out by one of the corrections officers that I'm gonna be leaving to go back to Miami in a few days."

"Did the CO tell you what day they were taking you?"

"She didn't tell me. She really wasn't supposed to tell me I was being moved in the first place."

"How are you feeling, now that you know you're leaving soon?"

"I feel a lot of anxiety in the pit of my stomach, but I know I'll be all right once all of this is over with."

"As long as you keep thinking positive, everything will be all right," he said.

"Would you call my attorney and let him know the U.S. Marshals are picking me up and extraditing me back to Florida?"

"Sure. I will do it as soon as we hang up."

"Thank you."

"Don't mention it."

"Oh yeah, before I forget, call Carmen too and let her know I'm leaving the jail, so she can keep my grandmother informed about my whereabouts. Carmen told me over the phone last night that they wanted to come down to Miami and be at my trial, but their money wasn't right. I need my family."

"Yoshi, you don't have to worry about all of that. If you need them there in Miami with you, then I will make sure they get there."

"Oh my God, Mario! Are you serious?"

"Of course, I'm serious. Whatever you need me to do to make your life easier, just say the word."

Hearing him tell me that he would do anything for me had me on the verge of tears. I mean, I literally caught a lump in my throat. I barely knew this guy, and there he was acting like we'd been together forever. I swear I didn't know what I would've done without him. He was heaven-sent. I thanked God for him every night before I went to sleep.

"You are a good man, Mario. I just want you to know that when all of this is over, I'm gonna pay you back for all that you've done for me and my family."

"Nonsense. You don't have to pay me back for anything. All I want you to do is help me help you get through this whole ordeal, and then after that, I want you to say that you will be my wife."

"Baby, I would love to be your wife!" I replied with excitement.

"Ahhh, bitch! Shut up with all that bullshit!" a voice yelled from behind me. "That nigga is blowing smoke up your ass! He doesn't want you, for real!"

I turned around to see who it was. When I saw it was this big-mouthed chick by the name of Lois, I rolled my eyes and turned back around. I knew the best thing to do was ignore her. She was the cellblock bully. I knew she wouldn't dare lay a finger on me, knowing Tina would tear her apart, so I dismissed her little comment as if she hadn't opened her mouth at all.

Mario said, "Who is that talking to you like that?"

I could tell by his voice that he was really concerned. "It's nothing, baby. Don't even worry yourself."

She barked loudly behind me, "So you trying to say that I'm nothing?"

I knew she was walking toward me, because her voice sounded closer and closer.

"Is she talking to you?" Mario asked me. He sounded like he was getting upset.

I tried to block her out, hoping she'd get the hint and leave me alone, but she kept pressing me.

"So now you're ignoring me, huh?"

"Yoshi, what's going on?" Mario screamed through the phone. "Why aren't you answering me?"

"I'm all right, baby," I replied, turning the volume of my voice down a notch, but really, I wasn't all right. My nerves were shot to hell. I wasn't in the mood to have an altercation with this chick. Even though I knew Tina wouldn't let anything happen to me, I still refused to go through the motions with this lady. I just wanted to be left alone, so I could talk to my man.

But apparently Lois had another agenda.

"Bitch, you still ignoring me?" she roared.

I felt the heat of her breath hit the back of my neck. At that point, I was fed up. I couldn't stand there and continue to let her attack me the way she was.

By then, Mario was going crazy on the other end. I wanted to calm him down, but I couldn't focus on him and try to defuse the situation that was brewing. I decided to turn back around and face her head-on, but before I got a chance to do that, she reached over my shoulders and hit the disconnect button on the pay phone. My call with Mario went dead immediately.

I didn't say one word. I gripped the receiver of the telephone in my hand as tightly as I could, and when I turned around to face her, I lunged back and hit her across her face as hard as I could. I swear, I have no idea what came over me.

She stumbled backwards and almost lost her balance. I believe she was just as surprised as I was, because she looked at me like I was insane.

I stood there with the phone gripped tightly in my hand and waited for her to come back at me. It took her a few seconds to regroup.

She charged at me, but Tina came up behind her and threw her right arm around her throat in the form of a hook and snatched her backwards. "Bitch, where you think you going?" Tina growled.

Caught off guard again, Lois struggled to regain her balance. Tina was one foot taller and at least fifty pounds heavier than Lois, so I knew it would be impossible for her to get away from Tina's grip.

"Get off me, bitch!" Lois screamed.

Tina tightened her grip around Lois' neck. I heard Lois gasp for air as she belted out obscenities at Tina.

While Tina tossed her around like a rag doll, I heard a few of the girls yelling through the metal bars for a corrections officer to come to the cellblock.

"Deputy, it's a fight!"

I rushed toward Tina. "Let her go. Don't get in trouble for me. Remember, I'm leaving soon. So let them throw me in the hole."

"Fuck that shit!" she spat. "I want them to throw me in the hole, so I can get the hell out of this block."

I stepped to the side when I heard footsteps running toward

our cellblock. I knew, at any moment, we were going to be put on lockdown, and the corrections officers weren't going to show any mercy on us.

"Everybody, get down on the floor right now!" a male officer yelled.

I turned around and saw one female and four male COs running toward us in riot gear and pepper spray in their hands. I immediately got down on the floor. Tina wouldn't let Lois go. She looked like Jill Scott beating down Jada Pinkett Smith. Lois was defeated from the door.

When the COs realized Tina had no intention of letting Lois go, they rushed into the cellblock full force and, when they got within an arm's length of Tina, unleashed what seemed like every ounce of pepper spray in the case.

I looked up and noticed that Lois had covered her face with her arms to prevent the spray from getting anywhere near her. Tina got burned pretty badly. I assumed the spray got in her mouth first, because she started coughing and spitting at the same time. When she finally released Lois, one of the COs grabbed Lois and threw her down to the floor, while the other two wrestled Tina down to the floor. It had gotten messy.

Tina was screaming and yelling about how badly the pepper spray was burning her eyes and her mouth. I felt sorry for her because if it weren't for me, she wouldn't have been in the situation. After the corrections officers took control of the situation, they hauled Tina and Lois out of the cellblock.

Lois snapped, "What the fuck y'all taking me for? This bitch is the one who hit me first."

"Yeah, why you taking Lois out the block?" one chick yelled.

"That bitch Yoshi is the one who started it. She hit Lois in the face with the phone."

The two COs left in the cellblock both looked at me.

"Is that true?" one asked me.

"She disconnected my call when I was on the phone."

It didn't matter though, because I'd physically assaulted Lois first. So, without hesitation, one of the COs handcuffed me and escorted my ass out of the cellblock behind Tina and Lois.

I heard those dumb-ass bitches laughing and cheering as I exited the block. They had no idea I wanted to leave the cellblock anyway. With Tina being gone, I had no one to protect me, so I wanted nothing else but to be taken away. Those hoes in there probably would've jumped me and beat the shit out of me if I was left inside that cage with them. God knew I wouldn't have been able to fight all those tramps by myself, so I welcomed being thrown in the hole. I didn't have much time left in that hellhole, so I could have cared less if I was thrown into solitary.

After everything settled down, I was locked away in solitary confinement. CO Dutton came by to check on me. When she appeared before the metal steel door and pulled back the metal slide window to peer through the glass, I smiled instantly. I was glad to see her.

"Are you all right?" she asked me.

I stood up from the bottom bunk and rushed toward the door. "Yeah, I'm all right. Will I be held here because of what happened back in the cellblock?"

"What do you mean?"

"I'm sure you know that I hit one of the inmates in the face with the telephone, so will that keep me from leaving with the U.S. Marshals?"

Mrs. Dutton laughed. "No. We can't hold you. Your paperwork has been processed and cleared by the warden of the jail, so you will still be leaving as soon as your name is called."

I let out a sigh of relief. "Good."

"What happened back there?"

"I was on the phone minding my business, and out of the blue that crazy-ass chick Lois came up behind me and started talking trash. I ignored her in the beginning, but when she reached over my shoulder and hung up my call, I went berserk on her butt. I turned around and hit her across her face as hard as I could."

"Well, how did Tina get involved?"

"Well, when Tina saw Lois getting ready to charge after me, she jumped in it and grabbed her—How is she anyway?"

"Who? Tina?"

"Yes."

"Oh, she's fine. They took her to the medical ward so they could spray her down with water to stop the sting from the pepper spray."

"What's gonna happen to her afterwards?"

"She's gonna get written up, if that's what you wanna know. She may even get some of her privileges taken away too."

I shook my head in disbelief. "It's all my fault. If I hadn't hit Lois, to begin with, then Tina would not have jumped to my defense."

"I understand what you're saying, but at the end of the day, Ms. Elroy is a grown woman. She made the decision on her own to attack the other inmate, so don't sit around here and beat yourself up about it. Ms. Elroy isn't a saint, you know. That lady's been in and out this jail for the past ten years, so believe me, she's prone to get into anything."

I stepped away from the door and took a seat back down on the bunk. I sighed.

"She is going to be all right. What you need to do is get yourself some rest because I'm sure tomorrow is going to be a long day."

I looked up from my hands and gave her a half smile. "Would it be possible if I could make a quick phone call to my boyfriend? I just want to let him know that I'm all right."

CO Dutton smiled back at me. "Yeah, sure. I can do that for you," she told me and walked away from the door.

A few seconds later, she let me out of that small-ass cell I was in and escorted me just a couple feet away to the pay phone. The phone call I made to Mario was very quick. I wasn't supposed to be allowed to use the phone at all, but she had talked to the officer on the floor and convinced him to let me make a two-minute call.

When Mario answered, I assured him I was all right. I asked him to get me something to wear down to Miami, so I could travel with street clothes on. He promised me that he'd make it happen, and he asked me to try to call him before leaving the jail. I told him I would try, and then we hung up.

CO Dutton locked me back in the cell and told me to take care of myself. I thanked her for everything, and then I told her to tell Tina that I wouldn't forget about her. She promised me that she would pass on the message, and then she slid the metal plate back across the glass.

A WEIGHT WAS LIFTED

A few days later, the corrections officer pulled me from that tiny-ass cell and escorted me down to the first floor, where the inmates were processed in and out of the jail. When he handed me over to a white man and white woman dressed dark blue jackets with the words *U.S. Marshal* embroidered in bold white letters, my case had officially been turned over to federal authorities.

Before I was taken out of the jail, I was handed a brown paper bag by the corrections officer and was told to change in the bathroom, which was only a couple of feet away from where we were standing. Without saying a word, I took the brown paper bag and went into the bathroom.

Mario had come through for me. It didn't take me long at all to change into the brand-new Nike sweat suit and sneakers Mario had dropped off for me.

Mario was definitely a sweetheart. He and I hadn't been together long, but my feelings for him had grown very strong. I had asked myself a few times, if I was really in love with him because of the genuine love he showed me? Or was it that whenever I was in a predicament he always held me down, even putting his life on the line? Did he just fill a void? Whether it was the first answer or the second, the fact that I felt that connection to him spoke volumes, and that was all I needed.

Immediately after I exited the bathroom, the U.S. Marshals handcuffed my wrists and placed shackles around my ankles.

"Ouch!" I bellowed as I looked down at the cuffs around my ankles.

"Are the cuffs too tight?" the female marshal asked.

"Yes. Can you please loosen them up just a little bit?" I asked.

Once she loosened up the cuffs, she stood straight up and placed her hand around my arm. She waited for her partner to give her the signal that they could head out.

"We're ready for the other inmate," the male marshal yelled at the corrections officers' station.

A female CO instructed another officer from the control room, "Open cell door four *D*."

Several seconds later the metal door let out a loud buzzing sound, and then the lock on the door clicked.

The officer continued, "Patterson, can you step out into the hallway?"

I heard chains slide across the floor as the male inmate made his way out of the holding cell. When he appeared from behind the beige-painted metal door, I immediately looked at him from head to toe. I had to admit, he was very easy on the eyes.

The male marshal instructed Mr. Patterson to walk toward us. The second he got within arm's reach of us, he was told to walk side by side with me and follow the lead of the female marshal.

While the female U.S. Marshal led the way down the corridor, all three of us followed. We went through several metal doors. When one shut, we had to wait for the other door to open. The security at the county jail was in full force. I couldn't see anyone escaping that place if they wanted to. Those country folks were on top of their game, and they made sure the inmates knew it.

After the last metal door opened and closed, we ended up in an underground garage. While we were being escorted to a white commercial van with tinted windows, I saw two uniformed police officers escorting a young guy toward the door we had just exited. He looked like one of your regular corner hustlers. His clothes hung off him, leading me to believe that he had been roughed up a little, possibly trying to resist arrest.

He gritted on the male U.S. Marshal and yelled out, "What the fuck you looking at, nigga? I ain't got shit you want, homeboy!"

Before the male marshal could utter one word, one of the uniformed officers yanked the guy by the hood of his jacket and told him, "Shut the fuck up."

Both marshals chuckled.

"I see you guys got yourselves a petty thug with a big mouth," the male marshal said.

"You're right about the big mouth part," the officer said. "But we busted this guy on concealed weapons charges. So you might be making a trip back this way to pick him up too."

The marshal smiled. "The pleasure would be all mine," he replied, and then he gave them a salute.

Five seconds later the marshal turned his attention back toward the male inmate and me. He opened up the side door to the van, grabbed a footstool from underneath the seat, and then told us both to climb inside.

"Be careful when you step onto the footstool," the female marshal told us.

Right after we climbed into the van and took our seats, the male marshal strapped us down in our seat belts, while the female marshal climbed into the driver's seat. This cat Patterson acted like he couldn't keep his fucking eyes off her. While he watched her, I watched him.

"Ready to get on the road?" the female marshal asked her partner.

"Ready as I'll ever be," he responded, and then he slammed the side door shut. He used a key to lock the outside of the door, and then he climbed into the passenger side of the van.

There I was, strapped down, handcuffed, and shackled, in a fucking U.S. Marshal van with metal bars protecting the window, like I was a part of a freaking chain gang. I was definitely out of my element.

But I couldn't say the same for this cat Patterson. His mannerisms led me to believe that he was a career criminal. He was super calm. I looked straight at his big hands and noticed the numerous cuts and scars around the knuckle area. Though he looked thuggish, he was handsome as ever. Plus, he was every bit of six feet, if not taller. His chocolate skin was so smooth, it looked like he wore some type of foundation. Even though he was locked up, his waves were spinning, and he looked like he took some pride in his appearance as much as he could while being locked up, with limited grooming resources.

There was nothing I liked more than a well-put-together man. I laughed at the thought of it, which, of course, got his attention.

With a look of aggression, he turned his focus on me. "What's so funny?"

I looked back at him. "Nothing." I then turned my focus to look out the window at the police vehicles we passed as the van exited the underground garage.

Silence filled the van as the sunlight beamed down on it. Both marshals pulled down their visors to block the harsh rays from the sun.

I looked at the time displayed on the dashboard near the radio dials. It was eleven fifty-seven a.m. That explained why the sun was shining so bright.

"There's nothing like a beautiful sunny day," Patterson commented, as he peered out the window.

Staring at the people going about their business on the streets, I quickly shared his sentiments. They were free to do whatever they wanted to do, and I envied them. Knowing that I may never be able to spread my wings again was a thought that began to cut me deep in my heart.

Thinking back to when I'd first purchased my penthouse in Miami overlooking the Atlantic Ocean almost brought tears to my eyes. I'd had it all—a great high-profile career; men at my disposal; a beautiful home and housekeeper; a brand-new Aston Martin; and a bank account with millions in it. But all of those luxuries had gone up in smoke. On top of that, I now had life imprisonment dangling over my head. If the attorneys Mario retained to handle my case didn't fight tooth and nail to vindicate me, I was gonna be forever fucked. And I couldn't have that.

As I continued to stare at the landscapes and the different cars we passed, I thought about how unfairly I would be treated once I returned to Miami. There was just no way I was going to get a fair trial, seeing that the media had painted me as a swindler and a killer.

While in deep thought I noticed the guy Patterson fidgeting with his handcuffs. He tried to do it discreetly, but my peripheral vision was working overtime. I turned and looked at him. He looked up at me and smiled but said nothing, so I turned back around and looked out the window.

"What's your name?" he finally spoke up.

I turned back around to give him eye contact. "My name is Yoshi," I muttered and quickly turned my eyes back to the window. Just like I suspected, that wasn't enough.

He asked me, "What's your last name?"

I gave him a seductive expression and said, "It's Lomax. Yoshi Lomax, Esquire. You ask a lot of questions. You work for the FBI or something?"

His eyes grew two inches wide. "You're a lawyer?" He completely ignored my sarcastic comment.

Before I answered his question about me being a lawyer, I looked at both marshals in the front of the van. I was a private person, and I didn't want them eavesdropping on our conversation. Thankfully they were in their own little world, listening to a country radio station and engaged in their own conversation, so I smiled at him and nodded.

He gave me an expression of disbelief. "Pardon my language— But what the fuck are you doing on this side of the fence?"

I let out a long sigh. "It's complicated." Shit, he wouldn't ever believe me. Most people didn't believe my story—high-paid attorney wanted for murder of a DEA agent, who just so happened to be her best damn friend.

"I'm sure," he replied, searching my face for an explanation.

"Enough about me. What's your first name?"

"Lamar." He smiled.

"Lamar Patterson, huh?"

"That's what I was told." he replied and then he smiled once again.

When he smiled this time, he spread his lips two inches apart from one another, so I was able to see his teeth. I noticed how white and perfect they were. I could tell he wasn't a coffee drinker or a cigarette smoker because the enamel on his teeth didn't look stained. They were absolutely amazing, and I had to comment on them.

"You have nice teeth." I finally told him. It was a left-field comment, but I just had to say something.

"So do you," Lamar replied.

I gave him a half smile and thanked him.

"How old are you?" I didn't hesitate to ask him.

"I'm thirty-eight. And what about you?"

"I'm thirty-four."

"Got kids?"

I sighed heavily. "Nope. I'm afraid not."

"Married?"

"No. I haven't crossed that bridge yet."

"You from Virginia?"

"No. I'm originally from New York, but I live in Miami."

"Whatcha doin' in Virginia?"

"Again with the questions," I looked him up and down, from his head to the handcuffs around his wrists.

He held up both of his hands with the handcuffs and the waist chains dangling. "My bad, Ms. Lady. Don't want no trouble!" he said and smiled.

Caught off guard by his little comedic act, I smiled back at him. "I'm glad you know what time it is." I commented and then I said, "I hate to get physical."

"You're a bad sister if you can do something to me while you got them cuffs on."

"Don't underestimate me."

"And don't you underestimate me." He winked.

Even though he said the exact same thing I said, the way he said it turned me completely on. It was the cockiness and the tone of his voice that got my attention. I'd always been a headstrong woman with a little bit of cockiness myself. When I run into men who are just as headstrong as I am, that says a lot for them. I was intrigued and I had to know where he was from.

"I'm from D.C."

"Oh, so you're from Chocolate City, huh?"

"That's what I was told."

"What got you down here in Virginia?"

"I was arrested here."

"For what?"

"You wouldn't believe me if I told you."

I pressed the issue. "Try me."

Before he opened his mouth to tell me why he got caught up in this jam, he hesitated for a second, I assumed to think of the right words to say. He let out a long sigh.

"I'm waiting."

"Let's just say that I was a bad boy," he finally said, a slick-ass smile spreading across his face.

I felt kind of guilty about thinking he was fine. Mario should've been the only man I was thinking about at a time like that. Especially because he was working so hard to make sure that I was going to be a free woman.

"Come on now, I figured that much out already," I replied. "I mean, you're acting like you killed someone." I raised one eyebrow just a little.

After I literally begged him to tell me what charges the feds had on him, he finally told me he got caught selling a ton of firearms to a couple of federal agents, and because of it, he was sentenced to forty years. His lawyer worked out a deal that he serve his remaining sentence in Miami, which was closer to his parents, who had retired there.

"Oh my God! Are you serious?" I asked him. This man was already sentenced. I knew one day I would be facing a judge to be sentenced too.

Instead of responding verbally, he nodded his head kind of somberly. Shit, he looked real sad, like his life was surely over.

I kind of agreed with him in my mind. Forty years wasn't shit to play with. I was taken aback by the severity of his punishment. I immediately reflected on my charges, and suddenly my whole mood changed. I felt like if he was caught selling guns and got forty years because of it then I was bound to get a life sentence for that bogus-ass murder charge they threw on me. Shit, I couldn't live the rest of my life behind bars for something I didn't do. This guy Lamar's life was turned upside down, and there wasn't a thing he could do about it. There was no appellate judge in the federal system that would overturn his conviction, not to mention his sentence. He was caught red-handed, so there was no if's, and's, or but's about it. He was done. I mean, it wasn't like he was T.I. or somebody famous who could sell a bunch of guns and use their money to buy a sentence of a year and a day. If Lamar was rolling like that, he wouldn't have been sitting there with me about to go up for a long time.

While I was dwelling on the possibilities of my fate, Lamar snapped his fingers to get my attention. "Ms. Lady, you all right?" he asked me.

I turned my focus back to him. "Do I have a choice?"

"It all depends." He smirked, all slick-like.

I shook my head as I turned my focus out toward the buildings we passed as we left the city limits of Chesapeake. Lamar must've figured I wasn't in the mood to talk about what was going on with me because in a low whisper he assured me that I would be all right, and then he fell silent.

Both U.S. Marshals continued on with their conversation. Periodically, I noticed the lady look at us through the rearview mirror, but for the most part, they blocked Lamar and I out. The guy kept her laughing at his corny-ass jokes, so she was well entertained.

After an hour into the drive, I noticed that we had entered on a farming area, where neighbors were about one to two miles apart. These people sat on acres and acres of land. Their homes sat back so far from the road, there was no question in my mind that they got in their cars and drove out to the main road to check their mailboxes. It was a place I couldn't fathom living in my former life.

This would definitely be a good hideout, though. Shit, I would surely convert to country living for freedom.

About a mile up the road I noticed that the van had slowed down. I leaned to my left and looked straight through the windshield and saw that we had come upon a railroad track. The gates were down on both sides, and the lights flashed on and off, but there was no train in sight.

I heard the female marshal sigh really loud.

The male marshal had a loud outburst. "Son of a bitch!"

"How long you think the train is going to be?" the female marshal asked him.

"I haven't got the slightest idea. You know this isn't my district, so you know I'm clueless about the country-ass transportation system around here."

As the van came to a complete stop at the railroad tracks, we all seemed to notice at the same time that a car was coming toward the railroad track from the opposite side. No one said anything about it, though. It was the only thing in sight for miles.

As we sat there and waited for the train to pass, both marshals grew impatient.

The female marshal sighed really loud. "When the fuck is this train gonna pass by?" She looked out the window back and forth up the tracks to see if she saw any sight of the train.

"There may not be one coming. Maybe this bar came down by accident or something," he replied.

And immediately after he made that comment, we all watched as the driver of the car on the other side of the track slowly crept around the railroad gates and eased across the tracks.

"What the hell is she doing?" the male marshal mumbled.

That was some bold shit the driver was doing by going around the barricade. Everybody in the South knew you weren't supposed to try to cross the railroad tracks if the pole was down to signal that a train was coming.

I felt like the whole scenario was strange. I could tell that a light went off in both of the marshals' heads as well, because both of them turned their attention toward the car and watched it as the woman behind the wheel drove by slowly.

Without saying another word both marshals followed the car with their eyes.

"I'm telling you . . . some people," the female marshal commented.

"Maybe she is in a rush. Shit, I'm thinking about doing the same shit."

All of a sudden we all seemed to hear a strange sound. At first I thought maybe the train was coming so the van was shaking from the vibrations, but then I realized it was a loud banging noise on the side of the van.

"Get the fuck out of the van!" I heard a man's voice scream out.

Then I saw the male marshal just disappear out of the passenger's seat like he was a part of a magic trick—*Shazzam!*—His ass was there one minute and gone the next. I screamed, and so did the female marshal.

She tried to go for her gun to help her fellow officer out, but she was too late. There was suddenly another man at her window snatching her ass out of the van too. I watched in shock. My heart beat so fast, it hurt.

I looked over at Lamar with a look of pure terror etched on my face. I was nervous as hell because we were helplessly shackled in the back of the van with no way to defend ourselves.

Lamar was unbelievably calm as shit.

The inside of the van suddenly grew overwhelmingly hot, and the air felt stiff. I heard another loud bang on the van, and I started saying a silent prayer.

This would be a fucked-up way to die.

Then the back doors to the van flung open.

I jumped so hard, I almost pissed and shit on myself. There were two men standing outside of the doors. They both had big-ass guns, probably machine guns for all I knew.

"C'mon, nigga, scoot your ass down here!" I heard one of the men instruct Lamar. It was clear that they knew each other.

Lamar scrambled his ass to the edge of the doorway, and the man with the gun helped him get out of the van. I was in fucking shock, to say the least. They were busting Lamar out. I thought for sure I had to be dreaming.

"Where this bitch come from, yo?" a big cinnamon-colored, grizzly bear-looking dude called out. He reminded me of Rick Ross, just a lighter version.

"I thought you said this transport was only going to be you?" the other guy asked Lamar.

"They threw her in at the last minute, I guess, trying to kill two birds with one stone. It's all good," Lamar replied.

"All good? Nigga, what we gonna do with this bitch? You gonna kill this bitch, right? We can't afford to leave no witnesses, *L*," the Rick Ross look-alike screamed out.

That was it, I almost fucking fainted right there in that van. Sweat broke out all over my ass. This man was actually talking about murdering me right then and there.

"Nah, just snatch her up. She going with us," I heard Lamar say.

A feeling of relief came over my entire body, and my nerves kind of simmered down a little bit.

It was obvious to me that Lamar had this shit all planned out. No wonder when I was talking to him earlier he didn't seem down or depressed like a man about to go to prison for forty years. This nigga was bold enough to have somebody breaking him the fuck out. Although I was scared, I had to have some sort of respect for that type of gangster shit.

"*L*, man, he's right. You takin' a risk on this chick. I mean, you don't even know this broad like that." The second guy was talking about me like I wasn't even sitting there.

"Look, y'all two, I said she comes with me—End of story!" Lamar gritted. There was complete silence.

The Rick Ross look-alike cat jumped up in the van and snatched me out like a little baby doll. "C'mon, bitch. One word from you and your ass gon' be on ice. You lucky he saved your life," he whispered, his thick weed-smoke lips close to me, blowing his hot breath in my face.

I wanted to ask his big ass who he kept referring to as a bitch, but I thought better of it.

The guy dumped my ass into the back of an all-black Tahoe with dark-tinted windows as the original car sat idle with the lady who originally distracted the marshals. I noticed Lamar was in the backseat of the Tahoe, while the other guy leaned into the car, helping him get out of his handcuffs and shackles.

Then the next thing I knew, darkness came over my eyes. They put a fucking blindfold over my eyes. I guess so I wouldn't see exactly where we were going. I mean, what did they think I was going to do? This was some serious shit I was into.

"Yo, be gentle on our little guest," Lamar told the Rick Ross cat.

I was happy he did, because that fucking Bryce was manhandling my nervous ass.

I couldn't see shit, but I could tell the vehicle had started moving. Then that's when I heard a lady scream and then the faint sound of gunshots outside of the windows. I knew right then and there that those two marshals were dead. I was too scared to ask any questions about where they were taking me and why. I was just grateful that Lamar had told them to save my life. I just wondered why he did.

THIS ONLY HAPPENS IN VA

I didn't know whether to scream for help or go along with all the chaos around me. It was like trouble just followed me, like I lived under a black cloud or some shit. I swear, if I could turn back the hands of time, I would. I had been through some shit, but this! The last few minutes seemed like something out of a damn movie. I had basically witnessed Lamar's men assassinate those two fucking U.S. Marshals. They shot the both of them in cold blood, I was sure of it. Neither one of them could have survived, judging by the number of gunshots I heard, and since they couldn't explain what actually happened, I knew in the eyes of the law I would be at fault for the murders just as much as Lamar and his crew. I was now an accessory to murder, on top of everything else I had on my fucking plate, especially because they didn't leave me behind as a victim; instead my fate was being on the lam with their asses.

With thoughts swirling in my head, I began huffing and puffing, literally about to faint. But I knew if I had said I needed air or complained in any little way they would've stuck the barrel of a gun up my ass. Bryce had already yelled at me once, so I wasn't trying to go back down that road again. I found out very quickly that I was in no position to call any shots. Nor did I have any control or say-so about where I was going. But one thing was clear: I was going with Lamar and these guys, and that was all to it. I didn't know if I was considered a hostage or what at that point.

I sat in the backseat of the Tahoe and remained quiet. I inhaled the strong scent of the purple haze they were smoking as I listened to Lamar and the other two guys talk all over each other loudly. The combination of the strong smoke and their loud babbling had my damn head pounding like somebody was hitting me with a hammer. I started to tell them all to shut the fuck up, but I realized that I was just a liability; if they felt like I would be a problem for them, then they would eliminate me on the spot.

Out of the blue while all of the commotion went on Lamar stopped talking to his friends and leaned back toward me. He apologized in a low whisper for the way his friend talked to me earlier. I gave him a fake smile through the blindfold that covered my eyes and told him not to worry about it.

"Are you all right?" he continued.

"No, I am not." I whispered back. Was he fucking serious with that question? I was blindfolded in the back of a SUV with some crazy bastards that had just killed federal law enforcement officers and was taking me to God knows where to do God knows what to me. No, I wasn't fucking all right!

"I'm sorry you had to witness all that," Lamar explained. "But we didn't have a choice. It was either them or us."

I swear I wanted to say something, but my mouth wouldn't move. I had a ton of emotions dancing around in the pit of my stomach. Plus, my heart felt like it had done a couple flips during the course of their escape and my abduction. All I could do was sit back and wait to see what the fuck was going to happen next.

"Ay, yo, *L*, what we gon' do with the girl?" I heard a voice yell out. It wasn't the same dude who had taken me out of the van; this voice was different.

Before Lamar answered him, I could tell he had turned toward me. Through the blindfold I could feel the heat of his gaze on me, but I was shivering like I was standing on a block of ice.

"We gon' shut the fuck up and keep driving. Where I go, she goes," Lamar hollered back at the dude.

Damn! I slumped my tense shoulders down from pure relief. I sat back with my lips sealed. I couldn't even make a comment about the dude asking what they were going to do with me, like I was a piece of trash or some shit. If I didn't go along with the silent act and just ride like I was doing, I knew I would end up just like everybody else these dudes had come in contact with—dead. They had already made it quite clear that if I didn't want to go along with them I wouldn't be going along with shit but the dirt of the earth.

Lamar kind of explained to me in so many words that they couldn't risk leaving me behind because they didn't know me and didn't trust me. They damn sure couldn't risk me making a deal with the cops to tell on them for my own release. Shit, given the fact that I was facing a life sentence, I damn sure would have negotiated a deal for my own freedom.

Lamar and his cohorts kept talking back and forth about my fate. Then I heard something that sounded like papers rustling. Next, I heard Bryce's annoying-ass voice.

"Yo, check this shit out. This li'l hottie we got with us is a fuckin' murderer," Bryce announced inside the truck.

Everybody all of a sudden got real quiet to listen to him read my card. My heart started beating fast. I was in disbelief. He must have taken my criminal file folder out of the marshals' transport van when he took Lamar's. Everywhere a prisoner went, those files followed them. I'm sure they took the files so that anyone who found the van wouldn't be able to figure out right away who had been in it. It made a lot of sense and would probably give Lamar and them the head start they needed to get far away before the authorities caught on.

I kept on listening to this nigga read all of my business out in the van.

"Whatchu mean, she a murderer?" I heard Lamar ask.

"It says right here—murder of DEA agent; evading arrest; conspiracy. They even got her marked as a previous fugitive from the law and a flight risk. I mean this chick got a fuckin' crazy rap sheet. We done picked up a ride-or-die bitch," Bryce said with a little chuckle, like he was amused.

"Yoshi, what's up with this, baby girl?" Lamar asked me. "I thought you said you was a lawyer."

I could tell he realized that I had been hiding something from him when we first started talking in the van. "I was set up. I didn't murder anyone. It's all lies, and I am waiting to prove it in a court of law," I said, hoping he believed me.

"Set up for the murder of a DEA agent? That's kind of deep, baby girl," Lamar said.

"I know, but it's true. The agent they are accusing me of killing was my best friend. I wouldn't have harmed a hair on her head. When I told you I was a lawyer, I wasn't lying. The setup was all because I didn't get an acquittal for a very dangerous member of the notorious Haitian mafia," I said somberly. I think Lamar could tell it was a sensitive topic for me, so he kind of backed off.

"I'm telling you, L, they really gon' be looking for this bitch now.

She is a high-profile prisoner. Which means she is a liability to us. We stepped in shit by keeping her," Bryce's monkey ass gritted out.

"It's all good," Lamar said in a low voice. He reached back and took the blindfold off my eyes.

I squinted to adjust my eyes to the light. Now that Lamar knew the real me, I was really wondering why he kept trying to save me and was being so nice to me. I mean, he could've just killed me with the marshals. I really had to wonder about his motives.

CHANGE OF PLANS

I read the green sign on the highway that said RICHMOND. I recognized some of the scenery. Then we turned off the highway. I was sitting up straight on high alert. Anytime we stopped, I was making sure they weren't pulling over to kill my ass and dump me somewhere.

The Tahoe came to a halt, and some of the guys, including Bryce, jumped out and rushed Lamar into this ramshackle-looking house. I could kind of tell we were in the hood part of Richmond by the looks of things. I thought about jumping out the back and making a run for it, but then I saw mad niggas posted up around the property and outside of the Tahoe and thought better of that idea.

I sat there until I noticed Lamar coming out of the house walking with much swagger. He had changed his clothes and was now wearing a nice-ass outfit that fit him perfectly. This nigga had even quickly gotten a fresh haircut and lineup. I couldn't believe he wanted to show his swag even though he was going to be on the damn run. I eyed him up and down. I was very impressed. He had on some True Religion jeans, an Ed Hardy T-shirt, and his jewels were glistening. I started wishing I could change my damn clothes too.

All of a sudden, seeing Lamar looking so smooth and together, I started thinking about Mario again. I was longing for a shower and a phone call to Mario. I didn't know when I would see him again, if ever.

I wondered if any prison officials had noticed that me and Lamar hadn't made it to the prison we were being transported to yet.

Lamar opened the vehicle door and smiled at me. He removed my cuffs and shackles. "You cool, baby girl?" he asked as he extended his hand to me as a sign for me to get out of the Tahoe.

I let a weak smile come onto my face too. I took his hand and I got out and stretched my legs. That is when I noticed they had a new car waiting for us—a nondescript midnight blue Dodge Charger. No big rims or real dark tints. In other words, nothing that would catch the attention of the police up and down the highway. We all loaded into the Charger and headed north out of Richmond.

While we changed cars and as we started down the road, I was still thinking about Mario.

"You cool, Yoshi?" Lamar repeated, this time using my name to address me.

Hell naw! I was thinking to myself, but all I could do was nod. My mind was racing with sad thoughts of missing Mario. What would he think when he came to see me at the new prison and I wasn't there?

Lamar, Bryce, and I were officially on the road again heading out of Richmond and out of Virginia altogether. After a few hours of driving, I fell asleep, my mind heavy with what-if's.

When I woke up, I saw the point of the Washington Monument getting closer and closer, and I knew we had made it to D.C. That's when I remembered that Lamar had told me he was from D.C.

"What's up, sleepyhead?" Lamar said, when he noticed that my eyes were open.

"Are we in D.C.?" I asked.

"Yeah. We gon' lay low around here until nightfall. We gon' park up at a little spot I know about where we can be safe until the sun goes down. Once we get to the spot, you better take the chance to shit, shower, and do whatever you got to do because we gon' be on the move again when nightfall rolls around."

"Where we going next?" I asked.

"We just gon' ride and wherever we end up is where we end up."

I knew that Lamar probably knew exactly where we were headed, but he wasn't trying to tell me. I think he must've forgotten that I'd heard him talking in codes to Bryce the entire ride to D.C. Now I can't tell you exactly what they were talking about, but I knew it had something to do with somebody from this part of town owing Lamar some serious cash. Judging from the urgency in his voice, I believe Lamar was trying to set something up so he'd be able to get the money while he was here.

I heard him say, "Bryce, now you know I ain't gon' be able to make a move without that paper, right?"

"Yeah, I know," Bryce replied.

I mean, it made perfectly good sense to me. He was on the run, and when you're on the run, you need lots of cash to stay hidden. But the questions that remained in my mind were, *What are his intentions with me? What in the hell is he going to do with me? Where the hell is he going to take me?* I was a serious target. I was wanted by both the DEA and the FBI, so I wasn't a good candidate to have around. Whether they knew it or not, they were playing a dangerous game by having me with them.

I was sure that by now my face was plastered all over every television and newspaper in the country, so it was impossible for me to hop on a flight, or even a boat for that matter. My chances of escaping to another country were one in a million, which meant I wasn't going anywhere, and if I wanted to stay off the radar, then I had to hide in plain sight. I couldn't tell how that would work out for me, but I didn't have a choice anyway.

Meanwhile, the other guy continued to maneuver in and out of traffic. Bryce's cellular phone rang. He looked at Lamar and nodded his head. Lamar in turned nodded back at Bryce. I guess that meant answer the phone, because that's what Bryce did.

After riding through some of the more classy streets in D.C., we finally arrived on a block that looked like shit. There was about five or six horrible-looking run-down motels next to each other. I looked out at a sign that read New York Avenue. I saw nothing but crackheads and dope fiends running up and down the streets. I looked around shocked.

"I know it looks rough, but this is my hood. Ain't shit gonna happen to you," Lamar assured me when he noticed my facial expression. Once again he was able to put me more at ease.

Bryce jumped out of the passenger side seat and went into one of the run-down motels on New York Avenue. Out of all of the motels on that block, the one Bryce went into was the best-looking one, even though it was still horrible-looking in my personal assessment.

Bryce was the one conducting the business of getting a room so Lamar could just go straight into the room and not have to see the motel clerk, who could later identify him if the cops got wind of Lamar's whereabouts.

Lamar reached over and patted me on the knee. "You look horrified. You ain't never been in the hood, Ms. Lawyer Lady?" he asked me, flashing that damn white smile of his.

"I've been in the hood, trust me. I'm good," I replied. I couldn't let the high-class Yoshi come out at a time like this. My life depended on just playing along.

Bryce came back with the keys to the room real fast. He jumped back in and pulled the car into one of the designated spots, then went and opened the motel room door so that me and Lamar could just hurry up and rush inside.

Once we were inside, I ran into the bathroom because I had to piss like a racehorse. The bathroom was so old-looking, I didn't dare sit down on the toilet. That shit had a dirt ring around the inside of the bowl, and the bathtub was in the same condition. The shower curtain looked like a relic from the '70s, and all of the tile grout was turning grey and black.

One thing was for damn sure. The cops probably wouldn't look at the old run-down motel for us. That's probably why they chose the place. Just seeing Lamar's swagger, I didn't think he would be caught dead up in a spot like that under normal circumstances.

As I continued to relieve my bladder, I could hear Lamar and Bryce talking outside the bathroom door. I looked around and noticed there was a small window above the tub. I thought about trying to climb out and making a run for it, but my thoughts were interrupted by banging on the door. I jumped so hard, I almost got piss all over myself and the floor.

"It don't take that long to take a piss!" Bryce hollered from the other side of the door.

I screwed up my face in disgust. This nigga was going hard, and he was crazy as fuck. A bitch couldn't even take a damn piss without him wanting to breathe up my asshole. It was clear that he didn't trust me as far as he could see me.

"I'm coming. I had to pee really badly," I said with much attitude.

Then I heard Lamar telling Bryce to be easy on me. That nigga Bryce hated my ass for real.

I came out the bathroom and didn't even look in Bryce's direction, but I could feel him eye-screwing me. He was a loose cannon. I sat down on one of the hard, dirty-looking motel chairs and folded my arms. I looked around the room, and everything looked run-down and dingy to me.

Lamar was smiling at me when my gaze finally landed on him. I sucked my teeth. He all of a sudden busted out laughing like I was a sideshow, or like I had told a fucking joke.

"What is so funny?" I asked him, annoyed.

"You look real cute when you pout. Your chinky eyes get even smaller," he said. "Don't let this nigga Bryce get to you. He is just overprotective of his boss."

That set my mind at ease a little bit.

Bryce had walked out of the room minutes before our conversation started, so I felt comfortable talking about my feelings to Lamar. "Why the fuck is he so mean to me? It's not like I exactly asked to be here," I snapped.

"Like I said, he is like a guard dog over me. My niggas all know if I go down for forty years they will not be able to feed their families. I'm their source of income, so it's a desperate time for these dudes. They would do anything for me, you dig?"

"Shit, I can feel that. I'm not trying to be funny, but I really feel like cussing Bryce's ass out," I told him.

Lamar busted out laughing again. He was laughing so hard, it was contagious, and it made me laugh too. I guess two fugitives on the run had to make the best of a shitty situation.

Lamar and I started exchanging funny stories from our jail stay before we came up for extradition, and we were laughing at some of the shit we had been through. We laughed and exchanged stories for a few minutes more, but that light moment didn't last long.

Pretty soon I heard the key turning in the door, and my mood kind of went back to serious. Bryce was back. He rushed into the room with bags of food and a couple of sodas.

Bryce's body frame was so wide, I didn't notice until a few minutes after he came in that a real pretty chick had come into the room behind him. I looked up and quickly noticed her striking beauty. She looked like she was of mixed heritage, like I was, except her looks were more like black and Hispanic, instead of black and Asian like mine. Her hair was pulled back in a long, pretty, jet-black ponytail, with not one piece of hair out of place. I could tell it was a weave ponytail, though. The chick was tall and wore flawless makeup. She wore a fresh American manicure on her nails, and I couldn't help but notice her long, pretty eyelashes from across the room.

She had a banging body too—an hourglass shape with a round ass to match. I could tell her clothes were expensive. The jeans couldn't be cheap the way they hugged her curves, and the pumps she wore were to die for. I could tell the large Gucci hobo she toted was the latest-season shit.

I started feeling a little jealous of her. I remembered a time when I could turn heads like this girl was doing right now.

At the mere sight of the well-dressed girl, Lamar jumped up off the bed, and I immediately wiped the smile off my face at the sight of her.

Lamar let a smile spread across his smooth face. He grabbed the girl and hugged her tightly like he had been missing her a lot. It was clear at that point that she was either his woman or his jump-off, but either way he knew her very well. His display of affection toward this beauty made me suddenly long even more for Mario's touch. I was envious as hell right then.

The girl kept her eyes on me suspiciously, and she didn't look at all happy to see me there. Lamar moved out of her embrace and went to introduce us, but the girl blurted her words before he could do the honors. "Who is this chick?" she asked him rudely.

I raised my eyebrows, about to let the real Yoshi take over. But before I could say anything to her rude ass, Lamar said, "Cora, this is Yoshi. Yoshi, this is Cora."

The girl twisted her lips, and Lamar pushed her into the bathroom so they could talk. I guess they were going to talk about me and why I was there with her man. So I was left in the room with Bryce's crazy ass.

Bryce put the fried fish dinners he had bought down on the little wobbly motel table. "Eat what you want," he grumbled, like he didn't want to feed me at all.

I didn't waste any time after he said that. I immediately started unpacking a Styrofoam carton of food from the bag. Shit, I was starving.

I could hear Lamar and Cora in the bathroom beefing. She kept saying, "that bitch this, and that bitch that."

I really wanted to tell her a thing or two about who was a bitch. She didn't seem to think Lamar was telling the truth about me being a prisoner that was being transported with him and having to stay with him to prevent having a witness against him.

I heard that bitch scream, "If she is who you say she is, just kill her!"

I couldn't believe my ears, but the food was looking too good. I started going in on the fried whiting and French fries Bryce had purchased. I noticed the arguing in the bathroom had stopped. The next thing I heard was the sounds of fucking coming from that little-ass motel bathroom.

Cora was saying, "Yes, daddy! Fuck me, daddy!"

It sounded like Lamar was letting that ho have it and making her shut the fuck up about me. I guess good dick will make a bitch forget anything, even another bitch. I just smirked to myself and continued to eat my food. But I had to admit, the sounds of fucking made me horny, which I knew I couldn't do anything about, so it also made me cranky as hell.

After their little escapade in the bathroom, Lamar and Cora came out. She appeared a little frazzled and not as perfect as she did when she first got there. Lamar looked satisfied, a big smile on his face.

Cora looked over at me and sucked her teeth. "I still don't understand why she going with you and I can't even know where you going."

Lamar started walking her toward the door. This bitch was overprotective of her man for sure. I watched Cora hand Lamar the keys to yet another getaway car. One thing was for sure: Lamar wasn't a dummy. He changed up shit enough, so nobody would get a good look at any of the vehicles we were traveling in.

Cora kissed Lamar deeply, like she was trying to prove a point to me, then she shot me another evil look.

Something about her gave me a bad gut feeling. I didn't tell anyone, but for some reason I knew her jealous-ass behavior would come back to haunt us.

"Do you need me to do anything before I go?" she asked him.

"Nah, I'm cool."

"Okay. Well, I'm just a call away, so let me know." She then headed for the door.

I was so suspicious of her that I peeked out of the motel window and watched her as she left. I noticed that she bent down behind a car and appeared to be doing something. Oddly enough, she didn't get in that car. I thought that was strange. I was hoping we never had to see her ass again, not only because she seemed like trouble, but she also reminded me of what I used to have and all the shit I had lost.

HEADING NORTH

It seemed like as soon as I had finally fallen into a deep sleep in that little-ass motel room, Lamar was shaking me to wake me up.

"Yoshi. We on the move. We need to bounce," he whispered to me and vigorously shook my arm.

I struggled to open my tired eyes. When my eyesight got focused, I could see that Bryce and Lamar were up and ready to go. I shot up in the bed and asked if I had time to pee and wash my face before we headed out. Lamar told me I could but that I had to hurry up because they had their time plotted out down to the hour.

Bryce was giving me the serious screw-face, like he didn't even want me to take a damn piss. As I walked to the bathroom, I looked over at the little dingy clock radio and saw that it was three o'clock in the morning.

After I hurried up and used the bathroom, Bryce handed me some shades and a Jackie O-style scarf to tie around my head for a disguise, just in case any nosy eyes were lurking. He pulled a fitted cap down low on his head and threw on some dark Marc Jacobs shades. We all left the motel room walking at top speed. Bryce and Lamar ushered me into the new getaway car waiting outside. The car looked familiar to me, though. Then I realized it was the car I had seen Cora bend down behind when I was looking at her from the window after she had stormed out of the motel room.

I started to say something to Lamar about what I had witnessed, but was too nervous because they were rushing me so bad, like they thought the cops were on the way or something.

We settled into the car and started up the highway. There weren't many cars out on the highway at that time of morning. I looked up at one of the signs and realized we were on the interstate, heading north again. I guess whatever business Lamar had in D.C. was a done deal, so now he was trying to find someplace to lay low.

Lamar sat in the back of the car with me. I took that as my opportunity to talk to him one-on-one without Bryce's interference. So while the music was up loud and I knew Bryce couldn't hear me from the backseat, I leaned over and whispered to Lamar, "Can I borrow your cell phone or any phone to call my man or even my cousins? I need to let somebody know I'm still alive."

Lamar looked at me with a pained look on his face. "I can't do that, baby girl. If you call your man or anybody in your family, we will be fucked," he explained. "By now the feds most likely have taps on all your family and friends' phones for sure. Those bastards are just waiting for you to call one of your close relatives or your boyfriend, so they can throw a trace or a cell phone GPS tracker out there. I'm sorry, I can't do that right now, baby girl. I'm real close to being a free man forever. I can't risk doing forty years. Plus, with this new charge for escaping, I would never see the light of day."

I don't even know why I was stupid enough to think Lamar would be willing to help me get in touch with Mario. I could feel tears welling up behind my eyes until they stung. I couldn't even imagine what Mario, Grandma Hattie, and my cousins Carmen and

Rachael were thinking about my whereabouts and my well-being. If the news story about the escape had broken in the media, they probably thought I was dead on the side of some road somewhere.

At that point, I didn't have shit to say to Lamar, Bryce, or anybody else for that matter. With the way I was feeling, I was liable to curse everybody out, even that crazy muthafucka Bryce, and I was kind of scared of his ass. I could barely keep still in the back of the car after Lamar busted my bubble by not letting me use his cell phone. I was sure he had those disposable, hard-to-track cell phones, so his dismissal made me even more furious.

Mario was all I had on my mind. This being-on-the-run shit wasn't going to work if I couldn't at least communicate with my new man. I thought about how thoughtful Mario was the last time I saw him. When he told me he had hired one of VA's hottest attorneys who was licensed to practice down in Florida, I was overwhelmed with joy. Mario had truly been a lifesaver.

The last time I saw Mario, he had assured me that I would be back in his arms in no time after the lawyer worked his magic. I should've known better than to believe anything good would happen for me beside meeting him. He was willing to stick by me even with the damn bounty on my head from the Haitian mob and the feds. I let out a loud sigh just thinking about everything.

"When the time is right, your family and your man will know you are safe and sound," Lamar whispered to me.

I guess he noticed that I was kind of sad and also a little mad at his ass. I didn't respond. I just folded my arms across my chest and went along for the ride.

"Yo, nigga, you a'ight?" Bryce called out to Lamar.

I scrunched up my face. Did he think I was going to do something to his precious boss? I looked out the window and started to see that the sun was beginning to come up a little bit. The dusky sky reminded me of Mario too. It was going to be one of those days when I wasn't able to get Mario off my mind no matter what I tried to do.

I was starting to hate Lamar and Bryce for putting me in this fucked-up position. Now, it probably didn't matter what lawyer Mario hired because I was once again considered a damn fugitive. There was no turning back for me. If I went back, they would surely throw my ass under that jail and throw away the key.

"We almost at the next spot," I heard Bryce tell Lamar.

"A'ight, nigga," Lamar replied. "Let's just keep making moves."

Although I was looking out the window, I could tell Lamar was staring at me.

AT MY WITS' END

We crossed the state line into Delaware. That much I knew. When we pulled up to yet another fucked-up-looking motel, I couldn't control my mouth any longer.

"What the hell is up with all of these hole-in-the-wall spots?" I asked Lamar. I didn't care at that point how he felt about my attitude. I probably would've even dared Bryce to say some shit to me, as frustrated as I was feeling.

"Well, it's not like we can walk up in the Ritz and say, 'Give us a room,'" he replied sarcastically.

I knew he would have a snappy comeback. I had learned that about him over the days we were on the run—He had a quick wit and smart-ass mouth.

"Yo, is this bitch about to complain? I mean, we can take care of that," Bryce chimed in.

"Fuck you, bastard!" I screamed at him. "Remember, I didn't ask to be here. I'm about sick of you calling me a bitch too! Do what you gotta do!"

As soon as the words flew out of my mouth, I regretted them. I must've been having a temporary moment of insanity. But strangely enough, Bryce kind of backed down after that.

Just like before when we'd stopped at the motel in D.C., Bryce hopped out of the car and went inside to get a room. When he came back, he practically dragged my ass out of the car, because I wasn't feeling it and I wasn't trying to move.

"Let's go, little murderer," Bryce commented as he grabbed onto me. When he pulled me out by my arm, he made sure I got a quick glimpse of his burner. That shit changed my attitude real quick.

When we got inside of yet another dirty, roach-infested room, I flopped down on one of the horrible beds and switched on the old-fashioned 19-inch TV. I needed something to take my mind off the situation at hand. Big mistake. As soon as I turned it on, the first channel I flipped to, there it was—two huge side-by-side mug shots of me and Lamar on the TV screen just as clear as day. The big caption on the screen read, "WANTED: DANGEROUS FUGITIVES."

I put my hand over my heart because I felt like I was going into cardiac arrest. I swear, I almost fainted at the sight of my face plastered on the news. Before I could alert him, Lamar noticed it too. Bryce was too busy talking to notice.

Lamar screamed at him and told him to shut the fuck up, so he and I could hear what the media had to say about us. That is when Bryce noticed what made us get so damn quiet. We all sat glued to the TV as the reporter spoke.

"In a brazen and murderous escape plot, two prisoners in federal custody pulled off a daring escape that ended in murder. Federal investigators report that Lamar Patterson and Yoshi Lomax murdered two United States Marshals and escaped from a transport van while being extradited from Chesapeake, Virginia to an undisclosed federal facility. Investigators further report that both Patterson and Lomax had been imprisoned for very serious crimes.

In fact, Patterson was set to begin a forty-year sentence, and Lomax was being returned to Miami to stand trial for murder of a Drug Enforcement Administration agent.

Investigators say during the escape Patterson and Lomax shot the marshals, a male and a female, in cold blood and escaped. Investigators also report that they do not believe the two fugitives acted alone during this heinous act.

There is a nationwide manhunt for Patterson and Lomax. Police are warning the public that this unlikely pair, a modern-day Bonnie and Clyde, is considered armed and extremely dangerous. The federal government is offering a twenty-thousand-dollar reward for any information that might lead to the capture of these two fugitives."

That was it! When that reporter finished talking, I completely fucking lost it up in that little-ass room.

I jumped up off the bed and headed straight toward the fucking door. "I'm out of here! Y'all just gonna have to shoot a bitch like me in the back. It don't make a fucking difference now no how! My life is over!" I screamed at the top of my lungs.

"Shhhh! Calm the fuck down, Yoshi!" Lamar grumbled at me in a harsh whisper. He placed his body in my path to try and stop me from busting out of that room.

"Move out of my way! I'm sick and tired of being on the fuckin' run! It wasn't my fuckin' idea to escape! Nor was it my idea to kill two marshals, but I'm being blamed all over the goddamn news. You can't tell me where we are going, and you have no idea how this is all going to end! So move the fuck out of my way. I am turning myself in!" I hollered.

I had dropped a bomb on their asses. Yoshi Lomax was not sticking around to have her name dragged through the mud again, being blamed for some shit she did not do. I was sweating profusely all over my body. My stomach was nauseous as hell, and at that point I honestly wanted to just go to Miami and go back to jail. If it meant for life, so be it.

I continued to push against Lamar to get toward the door. He was holding me in a bear hug. I can't front—His touch and embrace made me feel a certain level of comfort, but I refused to show him. I just kept on resisting.

"I am leaving! I cannot believe that on top of all the shit I have been set up on, now fuckin' with y'all muthafuckas done got me in a worse position than before! Move! I am leaving!" I continued screaming. I just lost it. I started fighting harder against Lamar's strong arms. Tears were running out of my eyes rapidly, and I started swinging on Lamar, punching him and trying to scratch his eyes out. At that point, I hated him for what he had gotten me into. I hated everything that was going on. I definitely hated that muthafucka Bryce.

"Yo, calm the fuck down and sit your ass down," I heard Bryce say, but at that point in time his words meant nothing. I was not in my right mind.

I kept on swinging, until I felt a force beyond anything I had ever felt before. All of a sudden I felt like my windpipe would just crumble under my skin. My eyes popped open, and I was face to face with Bryce's ugly-ass mug.

Suddenly I felt air under me like my feet were no longer on the floor. I realized then that he was holding me up in the air by my throat and squeezing it with one of his bear-sized hands. I struggled to breathe, and my legs were involuntarily kicking fiercely. I think my body's defenses were in overdrive. I started to feel lightheaded as this big giant strangled me.

"Bitch! You all in right now! You ain't turning yourself in shit. We let you live. You not fuckin' going nowhere until we say so!" Bryce huffed in my face. His breath stank of weed and alcohol. He kept squeezing my neck like I was a little chicken.

Shit was starting to get dark, and I knew I was going to lose consciousness soon. I could barely hear or see.

"Bryce, let her go! She just panicked when she saw her picture up on the news. She gon' be a'ight. Now let her go," Lamar instructed Bryce.

Bryce continued to squeeze my fucking neck so hard, I was completely unable to catch my breath. I felt like I was going to die. Slobber was starting to come out of my mouth at that point.

"This bitch ain't got no loyalty, yo," Bryce said. "She murdered her own fuckin' friend. Imagine what she can do to us if she got away. She can't live."

With shit closing in on me, I could barely understand his words, but I understood that he was trying to put me out of my damn misery.

"Nigga, I said to let her go!" Lamar screamed.

I could see out the corner of my eye that he had put something to Bryce's head. The next thing I felt was my body sailing through the air, and then I felt myself hit the fucking wall so hard, I could've sworn some of my bones cracked. I was on the floor hacking and coughing, or more like wheezing, to try to get some breath back into my body. I held onto my neck, trying to ease the burning pain I was feeling. That shit didn't help. My neck felt like it was on fire, and the inside of my throat felt even worse. I was sure I wasn't going to be able to swallow for a few days.

Lamar rushed over to check on me. He tried to help me up off the floor, but I had to get my bearings. My legs were fluid and slack like a pool of water.

"Yoshi, say something," he said to me as I continued to gasp for some much-needed oxygen.

I could hear the concern lacing Lamar's words as he tried to help and comfort me. He was a real gentleman, aside from the fact that he'd gotten me into all of this bullshit in the first place. I couldn't help but to start to feel for him.

He continued to ask me if I was going to be all right. All I could do was whisper, "I'm okay."

Lamar was finally able to help me up off the floor and onto the bed. I noticed Bryce pacing back and forth.

"Yo, don't ever do that shit again," Lamar told him with an angry tone to his voice.

"It's like this bitch got a spell on you or something, *L.* You better be careful of notorious ho bitches like her," Bryce replied.

At that point I could care less if he call me a ho, a bitch, a slut, or whatever. I just wanted to lie down. Not only was it clear to me that I wasn't going to be able to leave and turn myself in without a fight, it was also clear that I had to come up with a plan to save my own life.

Lamar comforted me until I fell asleep. He sat close to me as I curled up in a fetal position on the bed. He even occasionally rubbed my hair. It was definitely what I needed right then and there.

I tried to get an image of Mario to come into my mind's eye, but I kept drawing a blank. I was hoping that wasn't a bad omen—that I wasn't forgetting him—because that would've just been fucked-up.

▮▮▮

When I opened my eyes, it was a new day. I had slept for hours. I could barely swallow, and my body ached like I had been run over by a truck. Bryce had done a number on me.

I awoke to the sound of voices coming from the bathroom. I sat up slightly in the bed to listen in.

"Are they going to be able to get fifty thousand dollars for everything?" I heard Bryce asking.

"If you just stick with me, we gon' be a'ight. Nigga, I'm gon' be on a white-sand beach somewhere when it's all said and done. I'm telling you, it's like carrying a priceless diamond around. Those niggas know all about places far away that I can go. All they want is our precious cargo handed over," Lamar explained to Bryce.

I was intrigued. What the fuck was he talking about? *C'mon, Yoshi, you are smart. Think, think. What could he be talking about?* I was wracking my brain, trying to piece together the bits of their conversation I could hear. When I heard the doorknob turn, I hurried up and lay back down and pretended like I was still asleep.

"So we cool, nigga?" Lamar asked Bryce.

"Tu ferais mieux d'avoir raison sur ce point."

Bryce was speaking in fucking French. I couldn't believe that shit. It gave me a cold chill up my spine. I was wondering now if this nigga was Haitian or something. Lamar didn't ask any questions when he heard Bryce speaking another language, so he had to have understood what was being said.

At that point, I opened my eyes just in time to see them give each other a pound. I was curious now, but I stayed quiet. I acted like I thought they had just cleared the air. I mean, after all, Lamar had turned against Bryce to save my life.

Bryce looked over at me and didn't utter a word. He started putting on his sneakers and his fitted cap like he was going out. I was happy to see that he might be leaving. The tension between us was thick.

"How did you sleep?" Lamar asked me when he noticed that I was up. He seemed a little nervous when he noticed I was awake.

"As good as could be expected," I said in a low, hoarse whisper. My throat felt like little people were having a bonfire inside of it.

"Damn. I'm sorry about your voice. It may have been from all that screaming, though. You were straight wilding out," Lamar said. Then he chuckled because he knew he could always get me to laugh if he laughed first.

I cracked a small, phony smile. I got up out of the bed and headed into the bathroom. Something seemed a little funny, and I was smart enough to know it.

I stopped midway to the bathroom and turned around to Lamar. "The least you can do is try to get me a change of damn clothes already. I see your style and the type of bitches you fuck with, so I know you got good taste," I whispered, before turning and switching my ass in front of him while I walked into the bathroom.

I had been wearing that damn sweat suit for days now. Lamar looked like he had taken note of what I had asked him. *Fugitive or not, I still get what I want when I want it.*

"Oh shit. My bad, baby girl. I can hook you up. I'll have somebody bring you something nice to put on, you know, so you won't feel so bad about yourself," Lamar replied.

"Never that," I told him.

For the life of me I still could not picture my baby Mario's face. By now I was sure Mario had heard the news about the escape. If he believed what the media said, I knew he would hate my fucking guts for taking him on an emotional roller-coaster ride. But if he didn't believe the stupid-ass news reports and newspapers, then I knew he was sick to death with worry right now. Either way, it was a fucked-up situation for both him and me. I was wondering if I should just forget Mario and plan to live a life on the run.

I peeked at Lamar before I closed the bathroom door. *Damn, he really is a fine muthafucka.*

While I was in the bathroom I finally heard the door slam behind Bryce. I felt a little more at ease once that nigga wasn't around. Maybe Lamar and I would get a chance to have some good laughs like we had before while Bryce was gone. With that in mind, I hurried up and washed my face and brushed my teeth and got ready for a shower. I had to at least be halfway decent for the man I was starting to have feelings for.

ABOUT TO FLIP
THE FUCK OUT

After I got finished in the shower, I washed my panties out and hung them up in the shower. I threw my sweats back on with no underwear, so my ass looked extra round and plump. I came out with my hair wet and curly.

Lamar quickly said, "Damn. You look sexy as hell with your hair hanging down like that. I didn't know it was so long. Where is your family from anyway?"

"My mother is Korean," I replied. Then I noticed he was about to go into the bathroom. I immediately felt embarrassed. "Wait! Don't go in," I started to say, but it was too late.

Lamar rushed into the bathroom, which meant he was going to see my panties in there and know that I wasn't wearing any. After a few minutes he came out, smiling like a muthafucka. I had my arms folded across my chest.

"I guess you ain't want me to see your granny drawers," he said then he started cracking the fuck up.

"Nigga, Yoshi Lomax don't wear no damn granny drawers. Even under lockdown I was still rocking La Perla under my prison jumpsuit," I told him. I busted out laughing too. At least it took my mind off all the drama from the night before.

"You look damn good. I usually don't see chicks without all the fake hair and makeup on. I like natural beauty, though. Seeing you in the raw, no makeup and your hair like that, I can tell you are truly a beautiful girl."

Lamar then flashed that winning-ass smile again. I could not contain my smile at all. I was smiling so hard, my cheeks started to hurt.

"But girls who wash their panties out in the shower ain't such a turn-on," he joked, cracking up again.

"Well, you should get your goon Bryce to buy me some new drawers. That's if his ass knows how to pick them out for a woman. Shit, I can't see him even having a woman," I commented, laughing.

Lamar was rolling by this time, and in turn, so was I.

All of a sudden I heard a little thump outside the door and I jumped. Lamar stopped laughing when he noticed the strange look on my face. I silently hand-motioned and pointed to the door. Lamar looked over at it and then back at me.

Then there was another noise. We did hand signals for a minute, but neither one of us went over to the little dingy window to check and see if somebody was out there. We both stayed quiet. But after a few minutes of listening, everything was still silent. I exhaled, not even realizing I had been holding my breath.

"Okay. We have to keep our laughter and voices down now," Lamar warned after that.

I agreed.

After the noise, Lamar and I sat in silence for a few minutes, but we had such good chemistry that the silence didn't last long. We started talking again, and inevitably we were laughing again. I was sure if anybody was passing outside they would've assumed we were either fucking or having a hell of a good time in that room.

Lamar had the ability to take my mind off anything. For starters, I was still having a hard time even keeping Mario on my mind, and I damn sure couldn't picture his face. I was so conflicted about my feelings right then. This man had something about him that was so attractive. One minute I felt like I had to get the hell away from Lamar and Bryce, but the next minute I felt like I could go on the run forever and just forget about Mario, the trial, the Haitians, and all the rest of the trouble I was in.

"Damn! Where is Bryce? I'm absolutely starving," I told Lamar in between our jokes.

"This nigga be taking long as hell when he goes on runs. Maybe we just think he ain't got no bitches. He probably somewhere layin' it down right now," Lamar replied.

We both laughed at his joke. I couldn't imagine even the most desperate bitch giving Bryce the time of day. I was about to say something smart, but before I could say anything, I heard the doorknob click. I looked over at the door and got excited by the fact that Bryce was back with food.

The door didn't open up right away. It seemed like Bryce was having trouble with it. Lamar stood up and went to the door, so he could help Bryce with the bags and get the food faster. When he tried to pull back the door, he quickly realized it wasn't Bryce at all. Lamar came face to face with a short, stout Hispanic-looking woman dressed in a little pink housekeeper's uniform. Lamar stared at her and didn't move right away. She did the same. It was like they were both stuck on stupid.

"Ayi," the little Hispanic lady finally said, and then she placed her hand over her mouth like she was trying to keep herself from screaming.

The lady stood there staring at Lamar with a look of pure horror on her face. I swear it was like she had seen a ghost. Lamar was caught off guard as well. I was dumbfounded myself. This poor lady was probably just trying to do her job and made a mistake.

"What the fuck!" Lamar gritted, pointing to the DO NOT DISTURB sign hanging on the doorknob.

The Hispanic lady still appeared to be in shock. Then she said with a thick-ass Spanish accent, seemingly chewing on her words, "It is you . . . the man on the news."

"Bitch!" Lamar grumbled, and just as fast as he said it, he reached out and snatched the woman by the collar and dragged her into the room. The little woman tried to resist, but she was no match for Lamar.

As he pulled her in and prepared to close the door with the quickness, like a fucking nightmare, Cora came barreling through the door out of nowhere. It seemed like she'd just appeared out of thin air.

"Yeah, nigga! You didn't think I could hear you fucking this bitch and laughing with her!" Cora screamed.

It was like she didn't even realize that Lamar had snatched a poor lady into the room. She just kept carrying on about us being in the room together, but she immediately felt stupid when she saw that Lamar and I had on all of our clothes. She looked at me and then back at Lamar. I could tell she felt dumb as hell for her outburst.

"You dumb bitch! What are you talking about?" Lamar screamed as he held onto the wriggling housekeeper.

"She pay me open the door! Help!" the little lady screamed which caused Lamar to place his hands over her mouth and nose roughly. She was moaning into his hands and her eyes were as wide as saucers.

"What the fuck is going on?"

"Mind your fuckin' business, you bitch!" Cora hollered.

"Who the fuck you callin' a bitch? *Bitch!*" I spat, ready to floor her stupid ass.

"You stupid-ass bitch! You sent the fucking housekeeper to bust up in here? Do you know she recognized me? What the fuck are we going to do now?" Lamar said, still holding the lady captive for fear that if he let her go she would scream again.

"And I don't have to mind my business when you're the dumb, insecure bitch that put your own man at risk," I screamed over them.

"I just thought I heard you having sex with her," Cora said in a low tone like she was innocent.

I could tell she was feeling like the idiot asshole that she was right then.

"Now you gonna have to help me keep this bitch quiet!" Lamar yelled at Cora as the lady continued to struggle against him.

Lamar was sweating, trying to keep that little fat dumpling from getting away from him. I wasn't going to wait for Cora's dumb ass to get it together to help him do something with the lady. I started looking around the room for something to cover her mouth up with. Shit, my ass was at risk too, so I had no choice but to help.

This situation was more fucked-up than just being on the run. If that housekeeper got loose and went to the police on Lamar, she would tell on me too; especially for the federal reward money.

I finally found the scarf I had used as part of my disguise when we'd left D.C. I gave it to Lamar, and he used it and a rag to gag the lady's mouth so she couldn't scream. The poor little lady was crying hysterically and shaking all over.

I wondered if she had a family. I shook off the thought because I knew that there was a high probability that she would not be leaving that room alive. There was already enough murder and mayhem in my life, and now this.

That dumb bitch Cora was pacing around in circles while I helped Lamar bind and gag the poor lady. Here was another innocent person getting caught up in Lamar's escape plot all because he fucked with a jealous, dumb-ass young bitch like Cora.

As we tied up the lady, I eyed Cora evilly. I knew she was trouble from the moment I met her in D.C. I started thinking, *How the fuck did this bitch Cora know where to find us?* I wanted to know if Lamar was stupid enough to tell her our every move. I needed to find out if he really trusted her that much. I couldn't hold the question in.

"Lamar. Did you call Cora and tell her we were here?" I shot Cora a look because to me she wasn't worthy of any respect.

All of the color drained out of Cora's face like she knew right then and there she had been busted.

Lamar stopped and thought for a second. I swear it was like a light bulb had gone off in his head. "Naw, I ain't call her." Within a second, he was in Cora's face, breathing down her throat. "So, Cora, how the fuck did you know where I was at?" he gritted out.

It seemed like her words were caught in her throat.

Lamar grumbled, "Did you hear me?"

I just smiled and sat back to see what was going to happen to Cora next. She needed some consequences for her dumb-ass actions.

"I asked you, how did you know where I was at?" Lamar repeated.

I knew from how he dealt with his dudes that he wasn't the type who liked to repeat himself over and over again. That bitch Cora needed to start talking fast. She was already shaking, and her eyes were stretched wide. She knew she had no choice but to tell the truth. She broke down crying. Lamar was balling up his fist and gritting his teeth waiting for her answer.

ANOTHER BODY BAG

"I planted a GPS tracking device in the car I gave you when you was in D.C.," she mumbled.

My mouth dropped open in shock. I couldn't believe my fucking ears. This chick couldn't be serious. I knew she wasn't lying because I started thinking back, and now it all made sense. When I saw her bend down at the back of the car she had dropped off, the bitch was putting a tracking device on the shit. She was a fucking stalker. She was so worried about me, she had resorted to those fucked-up tactics. *Lamar's dick must be good to have Cora follow the shit from state to state.*

Lamar looked like he had seen the devil when he heard what Cora had done. He moved so fast, I didn't have time to blink, and Cora didn't have time to run or to even defend herself.

"I can't fucking believe you!" he screamed.

I could see blood rushing to his face. He charged over to where Cora stood cowering like lamb about to be slaughtered, and he slapped her across the face so hard, she lost her balance. She tumbled backwards and slammed into the small table in the room, sending the whole shit crashing down. All I could do was cover my mouth with my hand.

Blood shot out of Cora's nose, and one of her big gold earrings went flying out of her ear. Lamar had hit her so hard, she couldn't even get a scream out of her throat. I swear I heard her teeth click when he hit her too.

"All because you are a fuckin' insecure, childish bitch! You put my freedom at risk—Do you know that? You dumb bitch! What's wrong with you?" Lamar hollered, and then he hit her ass again with all his might.

Cora looked like she was about to faint from his hits. He was beating her ass like she was a dude in the streets. I swallowed hard and shook my head from left to right. It was a pitiful sight.

The housekeeper was moaning and crying as she watched the ass-whipping Cora got. I guess the lady knew that if Cora was getting her ass kicked like that, there was no telling what would happen to her. I guess she was losing hope for any chance of going free. She must've thought Lamar was a monster. I know I started looking at him differently at that point.

Lamar continued his rant. "I'm facing forty years, and maybe life now, and you playing jealousy games? Are you fuckin' crazy? A GPS? A GPS, Cora?"

Now he had a handful of Cora's weave and was wringing her head around like he was trying to take it off her body. Cora's face was twisted up in pain, a mess of blood and makeup. Her fake eyelashes were hanging off her eyelids, and she looked like an extra from a damn scary movie. I couldn't imagine how much pain she was in from getting hit with Lamar's huge, rough hands. As he dragged her ass down, I saw two of her acrylic nail tips go flying. I guess her high-maintenance style was out the window.

"Lamar! I'm sorry!" Cora cried out. She wiped blood from her nose with the back of her hand and tried to stand up, so she could get her hair out of his hands.

But Lamar hit her ass again, sending her back down on her knees. A scream got stuck in her throat, and she kind of gurgled from the hit.

I could see bruises popping up on her face from across the room. She was starting to look like a boxer at the end of a match. Damn, even though it was real fucked-up what she did just because she thought me and Lamar were fucking, I felt kind of sorry for her with the ass-whipping Lamar was putting down on her. I hadn't seen this side of Lamar yet. He was always so protective of me and cool, calm, and collected, even when Bryce got on his nerves. Shit, Lamar was acting like Cora had turned him in to the police.

"Why? Why did I ever trust you?" Lamar screamed, hitting her one more time for emphasis.

I could hear in his words that he was kind of hurt by what she did, because not trusting him was just like accusing him. Like most street cats, Lamar probably had a problem trusting chicks, and the mere fact that he trusted her and she betrayed him was burning him up inside.

Lamar finally got tired of hitting Cora, who was crouched down on the floor crying, looking like a pitiful heap of bruised-up flesh.

"I love you, Lamar. I just thought you were cheating. I didn't think the lady would recognize you. All I wanted her to do was open up the door. I'm so sorry. I swear, I would never do anything to hurt you!" Cora cried out.

That seemed to make Lamar mad all over again. I was thinking that Cora should've just shut the fuck up before Lamar came back over there and beat her ass to death this time.

"You don't fucking love me, you love the money! Don't get it twisted, bitch. I know the real you, you fuckin' hood rat ho. I made you!" Lamar yelled, veins popping out all over his face.

"I heard her in here giggling, and I love you so much, it drove me crazy. I could swear I heard the sound of y'all fucking. Lamar, you gotta believe me."

Cora's lips were swollen real big now, and her words sounded distorted, but I could understand her. I was sure Lamar could understand her words as well, but they did not matter to him.

"Just shut the fuck up right now before I tie your ass up too. I'm gon' let this nigga Bryce deal with your ass when he gets back. You know that nigga ain't all the way there in the head, so you better start praying, bitch," Lamar said coldly.

I knew he was mad if he was willing to turn that crazy nigga Bryce on Cora's ass. From what I'd seen and heard the few days I had been on the run with Lamar, it seemed like Bryce got a kick out of killing people, or at least hurting them real bad. I was already worried about what he would do to the poor innocent housekeeper who hadn't done anything wrong except cross paths with Cora.

I thought Cora should've been on her knees praying to God or any other higher powers that Bryce would have mercy on her when he got back. It was so much shit going on, I didn't know how things could get any worse at that point. As soon as the thought crossed my mind, I heard the key jiggling in the door. Bryce was back.

I closed my eyes and waited for the next set of drama to unfold. I kind of held my breath in anticipation of the madness that was sure to come. When Bryce stepped into the room and looked around, he dropped the bags of food he had in his hands. I could tell he was shocked by what he found. He looked around the room over and over again, taking it all in. Bryce didn't say a damn word, which told me he was processing the bullshit that was going on. My heart immediately started racing like a fast-paced drumbeat. I closed my eyes. I didn't think I wanted to watch what was about to unfold. One thing I did know, the shit was surely about to hit the fan.

GOTTA FIGHT BACK

"What the fuck is going on up in here?" Bryce asked as he continued to survey the room.

I cracked my eyes open just in time to see him looking at me. Then he looked down at Cora and over at the tied-up housekeeper. Then he looked back at Lamar.

"Yo, it's a long story. We gotta make some decisions, and we gotta make moves," Lamar told him.

Bryce walked over to the housekeeper and looked at her closely. She started to moan and cry louder, like she was begging him to help her. If she only knew, Bryce was the wrong person if she needed someone to help her. The mere look of Bryce and his presence near her was intimidating to no end. I felt kind of bad for her because I knew just how scary that nigga could be.

"Who the fuck is this?" Bryce asked. His face was crumpled up with confusion. He was absolutely in full disbelief. It was almost comical.

When he looked over at me, I lowered my eyes to the floor. I wasn't going to be the one to tell him what Cora did. I was staying way out of this little piece of soap-opera drama.

Lamar explained to Bryce, "This bitch over here hired the motel housekeeper to open the door with her master key. Apparently, Cora put a GPS in the whip she gave us. Then she downloaded the location of the whip, brought her raggedy ass here, and got this lady to open the door. What the silly bitch didn't realize was, my face and Yoshi's face is all over the media, and the fuckin' housekeeper immediately recognized me when she came in the muthafuckin' room with the master key." Lamar was getting heated by the minute as he told Bryce the story.

Bryce's chest starting heaving up and down, and I saw him bite down into his jaw. I recognized the signs too. That was that crazy-man shit about to come out, and I knew it.

"Nigga, you can't be fuckin' tellin' me the truth right now." Bryce cracked his knuckles. He looked over at Cora and back over at the housekeeper, who'd pissed on herself when she saw how big and ugly Bryce was. I was glad he didn't look at me for once.

"I wish I was lying. I beat this bitch to a pulp over this shit. Look at my knuckles," Lamar said, showing Bryce the scraped-up skin on his hands.

I hadn't even noticed his knuckles were all scratched from him hitting Cora so hard. One of his knuckles was even bleeding. He told Bryce he thought he hit Cora's teeth with that hand.

"They both gotta die. You know this, right?" Bryce said to Lamar.

Lamar had already anticipated that Bryce would say that. He sat down on the end of the bed and put his head in his hands. I knew that meant he didn't really agree with Bryce, that he wanted time to think. He had the habit of putting his head in his hands when he was plotting our next move.

"This is way too many bodies piling up, man," Lamar said. "I just wanted to get the fuck out of Dodge without adding to the death toll."

"We gotta do what we gotta do," Bryce said as he walked over to where Cora was curled up on the floor.

Cora saw Bryce coming, and she immediately put her hands up over her face in defense.

"You a stupid-ass trick, you know that? I should shoot your ass right the fuck here on the spot. I can't believe how fucked-up you are. You that dick-whipped that you would bring drama up here? I knew, when I met you, this nigga shoulda fucked you and kept it moving." Bryce spat at her, the ultimate disrespect in my book.

Bryce then took his gun out of his waistband and pointed it right at Cora's temple. She started trembling. I covered my eyes. I didn't want to see that girl's brains all over that room.

Lamar jumped up and grabbed Bryce before he could do something stupid like shooting Cora in the damn head. Cora had her eyes squeezed shut, so she didn't even really know Lamar had saved her ass. I guess she had been preparing herself to die right then.

"Look, nigga! Stop! We need to decide what our next move is gonna be! Calm the fuck down!" Lamar grabbed onto Bryce's arm.

Bryce held his gun on Cora for a long time, while Lamar kept demanding for him to put the shit away. I just knew I was going to see Cora's brains splattered all over that fucking wall. Finally, after about ten minutes of a little standoff between Bryce and Lamar, Bryce lowered his gun and put it back in his pants.

I just shook my head. This was some bullshit. It had to be better to be in Miami facing the music for my crimes than to witness all of this shit.

Lamar sat back down and went into thinking mode, his head in his hands for about twenty more minutes.

Bryce, on the other hand, was pacing the floor like the maniac he was. Then he looked over at the housekeeper with a crazy look in his eyes. She was fixated on Bryce, her eyes wide in fear. I guess she had given up on crying and trying to talk with the gag in her mouth.

Poor thing, I thought as I watched her.

All of a sudden, Bryce rushed over to the housekeeper and picked up the chair she was tied up in. Her body stiffened in surprise. The lady started moaning and trying to move her body in response to Bryce moving her.

"Shut the fuck up!" Bryce gritted. He put the chair in the bathroom and slammed the door.

We were all looking at Bryce like he was really fucking nuts. Nobody could understand why he put her in the bathroom or what she had done that made him do that.

"What the fuck y'all lookin' at?" Bryce grumbled at us. "She kept staring at me."

Lamar finally lifted his head up from his hands. He suggested, "Yo, maybe we can just knock her unconscious and get the fuck out of here. By the time she wakes up, we'll be long gone."

"Yeah, I think that is the best. That lady ain't do shit to deserve to die," I said, adding my two cents to the matter.

"No! She saw my face. I'm a fuckin' accomplice to all this bullshit. Nigga, if you don't care about going to back to jail for forty years, that's you. But I ain't doing no bid for helping you escape. I'm damn sure not going down for the murder of two marshals. The bitch gotta die, and that's final."

"Do you see what you did, Cora?" Lamar hollered to Cora, who was just rocking back and forth crying.

"I feel like throwing you off a fuckin' bridge, Cora, for real," Bryce said.

Lamar looked stressed as hell. He started pacing. This shit was getting on my fucking nerves now. Either these niggas were pacing or cussing or killing some fucking body. I kept contemplating making a run for it out of the door while they were distracted, but I remembered I didn't know my way around Delaware, and I didn't have a fucking red cent to my name. They don't transport prisoners with money in their damn pockets.

"A'ight. If you gon' kill the fuckin' lady, it can't be in here. We're gonna have to take her out of this room. We can't risk having a murder in a room that you got with your ID. Even if it's fake and has somebody else's government name on it, it's still your fuckin' picture. When we break out, if they find a body up in here, the police will pull the copy of your ID from the clerk's office. Then they'll be looking for your face too, nigga, so let's think this shit through," Lamar explained to Bryce.

I could tell Lamar was conflicted and confused.

"That's what I'm talkin' about, nigga. You thinking like me now," Bryce said excitedly.

I knew this muthafucka got his rocks off on killing people.

"Just remember this shit gotta be as quiet and as clean as possible," Lamar instructed.

Lamar had given in. There was going to be yet another dead person in our wake.

"Yeah, I got you. After I do the deed, we gonna have to get the body the fuck up out of here as soon as it gets dark. Then we gon' decide what the fuck to do with that dumb bitch over there," Bryce said, pointing to Cora.

I felt cold creep all over my body. I couldn't believe they were actually going to kill that innocent woman. I was disgusted with Lamar for not standing up for shit. I was sure if they had threatened her good enough with Immigration or some shit, that little lady would've gone about her merry way and never said a word about seeing us.

"You a triflin' bitch, Cora!" I yelled. "I can't believe you got this lady into this shit, and you just sitting here like nothing is about to happen. You think I'ma fuck a dude that kidnapped my ass from a prison van? I don't want your fuckin' man. What I want is to go the fuck back to Miami."

Lamar and Bryce were both looking at me like I had lost my mind. At that point, I did not care what the fuck they thought about me. I just could not hold it back any longer. I wanted to beat that bitch up all over again for this bullshit. Lamar looked like he was a little disappointed that I'd told Cora I didn't want his ass. It was true right then. All the attraction I had started to feel for him was fading fast.

"Shut the fuck up!" Cora told me out of her busted-up lips. "If it wasn't for you, this would've never happened. You giggling with Lamar and making it seem like something was going on. You don't know me, or what I been through with this nigga."

I really could care less what she'd been through. I folded my arms across my chest and cocked my head to the side. I told that bitch, "No, *you* ought to grow the fuck up, and if your man is a cheater, get a fuckin' new one."

"Fuck all of this! It's time to get this shit done." Bryce headed into the bathroom, where the poor little Mexican housekeeper was still sitting tied to the chair. All I could do was shake my head, because I knew what was going to happen to her next.

Bryce closed the door behind him when he went inside the bathroom. I could've sworn I saw a small smile on his wicked-ass face. The next thing I knew, I heard a lot of bumping and moaning coming from inside the bathroom. Then I heard a big thud. It sounded like he had slammed the lady on the floor or into the bathtub.

I heard a gagging sound, and I placed my hands over my ears. I did not want to listen as that lady was murdered for no fucking reason at all. There was a bunch of loud thumping coming from the bathroom, but oddly enough, there were no screams.

Lamar jumped up and headed into the bathroom to see what exactly was going on. He hesitated, but he went inside anyway. When he opened the door, I caught a glimpse of what was going on inside. Bryce had the woman in the bathtub and was over her, strangling her with his bare fucking hands. The lady was fighting for her life for a minute, her arms flailing and all that.

I turned my head away when I saw Bryce look up with a big smile on his face as he continued to squeeze her neck mercilessly. I think I heard a couple of bones in her neck snap after a while. Bryce was actually enjoying it.

Cora was crying. I truly could've slapped the living shit out of her right then. It was too late to be fucking crying after all that trouble for nothing. Lamar was just standing there watching the murder unfold because that was all they could do to protect his freedom.

When the noises and bumping finally stopped, I knew then that the lady was finally dead. My next thought was, *What the hell are they going to do with her body?*

"It's all done. Once again I cleaned up everybody else's fuckin' mess!" Bryce growled. He really looked like an animal. His face and neck was covered in sweat. His hands were balled into fists. Bryce resembled a beast that had just killed its prey. He was huffing and puffing and shit. I felt like I was watching a horror flick.

Lamar just sat back down in his usual position with his head in his hands. Frankly, I was sick and tired of seeing him sitting like that. It made him look weak as hell to me.

"Somebody gonna have to help me get this body out of here tonight," Bryce announced.

The thought of being in the same room with another dead body made me want to throw up. Seeing my murdered friend Maria in the state that she was in when I'd found her was enough death up-close to last me a lifetime. Now this one was the topper.

I squinted at the evil bastard Bryce, and then I looked over at that bitch Cora too. "You should make Cora help you," I blurted out. It was like the words just leaked from my mouth before I had even thought about it.

"No. I'm still deciding if I'm going to even let Cora live," Bryce commented, cracking his knuckles for the tenth time.

He was serious as hell too when he said he didn't know if Cora was going to live. Cora was dead silent. In fact, after Bryce made his comment, the entire room was quiet. Death was definitely in the air.

I didn't even have an appetite to eat the food Bryce had brought back with him. I already had it planned out that as soon and he and Lamar left the room to take the body out, I was going to try to see if I could use the phone to call Mario or one of my cousins. Somebody was going to have to try to save me from all of this bullshit.

Bryce went back into the bathroom and asked Lamar to follow him. I was listening to them as hard as I could. That's when I could've sworn I heard Lamar speaking French too. That shit was starting to freak me out.

Then they both came back out of the bathroom. Bryce walked over to Cora, grabbed her by her hair, and dragged her over to the chair he had brought back out of the bathroom. He forcefully put her in the chair.

"Lamar, please don't," Cora cried all over again. "I'm sorry." She tried to get up out of the chair, but Bryce forced her back down with his strong arms.

Lamar walked over to her, and they began tying Cora up just like we had done to the housekeeper.

PLAYING DIRTY

I t seemed like nightfall would never come as we waited for it to get real dark so they could get rid of the body and we could get the fuck out of Dodge. The sun was still peeking out of the clouds, which meant we still had to sit there with a dead body right in the bathroom.

Cora had given up on fighting or trying to call out to Lamar to beg for his sympathy so he would untie her. Her ass was tied up, and that was the final say.

I was jittery as a fucking jumping bean. Every little noise made me jump. But nothing could prepare any of us for the nervousness we felt when we heard a damn knock on the door.

"Marisol? Marisol!"

Whoever it was also had a Spanish accent, and she was frantic as hell calling out the name "Marisol."

"Who the fuck is that?" I exclaimed, worry all over my face. I mean, there was a fucking dead body right in the bathroom!

"Be calm. Everybody, stay fuckin' calm," Lamar instructed, putting his hands up for emphasis. He snuck over to the window and peeked out with one eye. "It's another housekeeper," he whispered in a panicky tone.

I saw Lamar's hands kind of shaking. Fuck that, I didn't know about him, but my entire body was shaking.

"Fuck!" Bryce whispered.

"Cora, you are going to have to go to the door. Act like you in here getting busy with your man or something, so you can get rid of her fast. And don't try no funny shit, or I will shoot you and her too," Lamar whispered gruffly.

He and Bryce started untying Cora. I couldn't go to the door for fear that the lady would recognize me just like the dead housekeeper had recognized me and Lamar.

The lady on the other side of the door continued to knock and call out her friend's name. "Marisol! Marisol!" she yelled, and each time she did, her voice got louder and louder.

When Cora was loose, Bryce helped her out of the chair. He grabbed her arm roughly and walked her over to the door with his gun stuck in her back up against her spine. Cora just followed along and did as she was told. She didn't have much of a fucking choice either.

"Crack the door open just enough so you can peep out the door," Bryce instructed. "I don't want her to see your face. And make it quick, so she can carry her ass."

Cora opened the door a small crack and stuck her face into the crack, so the lady couldn't see inside of the room, or what a wreck she was. "Can I help you? We have the do-not-disturb sign on the door," she told the lady in a fake annoyed tone.

"I'm looking for my friend, Marisol. She is the housekeeper. She come in this room," the other housekeeper told Cora.

"No, she didn't."

"Yes, I see her come in this room. I see you talkin' to her earlier.

She no come with you to this room?" the lady told and asked Cora at the same time.

I knew Cora felt like fainting from her nerves. That lady had actually seen the dead housekeeper speaking with Cora. She also probably saw her friend open up the door with the key and get snatched inside.

"No. We were talking. I did ask her one question. But she did not come in here with me, and I haven't seen her since I came inside the room. I am in here with my man, if you don't mind."

"No. She come in here. I think I see her follow you," the lady insisted, straining to see behind Cora. She would not give up.

"Look! I told you I only asked her one question, and she left. She is not here, and I have business to take care of with my man," Cora hollered at the lady. She started to shut the door in the lady's face.

"I gon' call the police. Marisol did talk to you. She came in here. I know it," the lady told Cora.

When I heard her say she would call the police, I just let out a long sigh.

"Bitch, get away from this door! You send the fuckin' police here, and I will have your wetback ass fired immediately." Cora slammed the door in the lady's face.

When Cora turned around, I could see the stress on her face, Lamar breathing down her neck.

"What now?" Lamar asked. "The lady is going to call the police and send them to this room. What the fuck are we going to do?"

I just wanted to get the fuck out of that room. I didn't care if I had to walk two hundred miles. At that point I would've done it.

"We gotta get this body out of here right fuckin' now!" Bryce screamed.

We all looked over at the window at the same time and noticed that the sun was finally beginning to go down, which meant the time to be on the move was approaching us real fast.

Bryce started getting prepared. He walked over and snatched the blanket off one of the beds and headed into the bathroom. Lamar headed in behind him.

I turned my face away when I saw them hoist the housekeeper's limp body out of the bathtub. As much as I didn't want to look, I couldn't help it. I peeked into the door and instantly felt sick to my damn stomach. The lady's eyes protruded out of her face like she was a cartoon character. Her tongue was hanging at the side of her mouth too, and it looked swollen. Her skin looked a little blue around the neck area.

I tried not to look, but curiosity got the best of me. When I opened my eyes, I noticed that Bryce and Lamar had wrapped the poor lady's body in the blanket like she was a piece of trash.

Lamar was shaking his head in disgust. I knew he didn't want to murder that lady, but what choice had Cora left him?

"Yo, Cora, go and check out what's going on outside," Lamar told her. "Make sure no one is out there."

"You trustin' this bitch again?"

Bryce said just what the fuck I was thinking. Why would Lamar trust her to do shit for him? If it was up to me and Bryce, Cora's ass would've been tied right back up after the other housekeeper left from the door. That bitch was not to be trusted at all.

"What choice do we have? It's not like we can send Yoshi. Her fuckin' face is all over the news just like mine!" Lamar replied.

Cora went over to the window and looked out. "I don't see anyone. The parking lot looks empty," she whispered.

"Are you sure the parking lot is empty? We can't be taking chances of being caught. We need to be able to make a straight beeline to that fuckin' car real fast," Lamar told her.

Cora was anxious to do what she was told, like a ready soldier.

"And don't try no funny bullshit, or else we will be getting rid of two fuckin' bodies," Bryce warned her.

Cora knew he was serious too. She walked slowly and nervously. She opened the door and stepped outside to look around. Then she rushed back into the. Her eyes were wide, and she was breathing hard as hell too. She looked like she had seen a ghost or something.

"What's going on?" I asked her.

Cora gathered her breath. Then she swallowed hard and tried to speak fast through her swollen lips. "There are cops all over the place out by the front lobby door," she said. Her chest was going up and down like she had just run a half marathon.

"Where are they? Fuck! What the fuck now!" Bryce exclaimed, throwing his hands up. It was obvious his big goofy ass had a fear of going to prison. Any mention of cops, and that nigga started coming apart at the seams.

"I can't believe that a big guy such as yourself is afraid of the police." I smiled.

Bryce's face almost exploded. His eyes damn neared popped out of his head. "Who the fuck you think you're talking to, you dizzy-ass broad? Do you know I will kill a fuckin' cop in a heartbeat? I went to prison for gunnin' at a couple of police in a cop car. So don't come at me with that disrespectful shit ever again."

"Just, everybody, calm down! We have to come up with a plan." Lamar once again put his head in his hands and went into deep thought. "It's going to be all right." His words sounded uncertain.

I don't even know why Lamar said some bullshit like, "It's going to be all right," because he didn't believe that shit himself. Dead bodies and cops don't mix. And then when you throw in two fugitives from the law, you damn sure got a fucked-up scenario.

I was pacing around in circles. I didn't care what they did with the body. What I cared about the most was trying to figure out if I was going to make a run for it when Lamar and Bryce left to get rid of the body. Shit, I had to get the fuck away from them. Being with them caused me to be an accessory to three murders. I was already being portrayed as a triple murderer and a fugitive from the law on the news and everywhere. This was some straight-up bullshit. Like a bad dream you can't wake up from.

I kept eyeing all three of them. I had been making mental notes on who was smart, who was straight fucking dumb, and how I could use their weakest points against them.

"How the fuck are we gonna get out of here with this body with cops all over the place?" Bryce asked Lamar.

Bryce was being impatient, and his mood was making the panic in the room magnified. Even I wanted to slap him and tell him to calm the fuck down.

"We gon' stay calm, and shit gonna work itself out," Lamar said, extra calm as usual.

Too fucking calm, if you ask me.

Soon as Lamar said what he said about shit working itself out, we heard the cops going door to door to ask guests in the motel if they had seen the missing housekeeper. We all had a look of horror on our faces. It would be just a matter of time before the cops got to our door to ask about Marisol.

ENOUGH IS ENOUGH

Lamar and Bryce rushed back into the bathroom and put the body back into the bathtub and pulled the shower curtain closed before the cops got to our door. Me and Lamar had to stand in the bathroom and hide too because none of us knew if the cops were going to ask to "take a look around," like they usually did in the hood. The plan was to have Cora and Bryce act as if they were a couple until the cops left.

Before I went into the bathroom to hide, I saw Bryce taking off his clothes. That grizzly, hairy-ass nigga stripped down to his boxers. He made Cora strip down too, and she got into the bed and pulled the cover just around her breasts and played sleep, hiding her face with her arm. That was fast thinking on his part. I figured out that Bryce wanted him and Cora to act like they had fucked until they were tired, so the cops wouldn't even suspect that the housekeeper was in our room.

We all waited for the impending knock on the door. Sure enough, after about ten more minutes, the cops knocked on the door to our motel room. The sound of the loud knocks made me jump, even though I was in hiding.

Lamar noticed my nervousness and held me. "Shhh, it's gonna

be all right," he whispered in my ear. "We gon' get out of here, and as soon as we do, I will let you call your grandmother and your cousin."

I don't know why, but I was instantly comforted by him. His breath made a hot feeling travel down my spine. At that moment, I just melted in his arms. I really wanted to believe that he would let me call some of my family. But my moment of calm didn't last long. When I opened up my eyes from my fantasy and looked down at the dead housekeeper's face showing a little bit from under the blanket, I immediately felt like throwing up. I hid my face in his chest anyway.

"Hi, officer, is there a problem?" I heard Bryce say.

"Hi, sir. We need you to help us out. We are looking for this woman. Have you seen her?" the cop asked.

I could picture the cop showing Bryce a picture of the housekeeper who was dead at my fucking feet right at that moment.

"Nah. I'm sorry. We came straight in here and crashed." Bryce let out an exhale. "You can come in and take a look around if you want."

I could hear some quick movement inside. I felt the officers' presence and my heart raced. I thought any second he would pull back the shower curtain and we'd all get busted and I didn't want to go to jail for some shit I didn't do. I figured I would need to get away from their asses so that I could tell my side of the story. "Thank you. And I apologize for the inconvenience," I heard the officer say.

The next thing I heard was the door slamming. Bryce's plan had worked. I guess he was smart after all. When I was sure the cops were gone, I moved away from Lamar. We had gotten through a very close call on that one. Now it was going to be time to make power moves, and I knew it. Our softest moment was all over. It was back to being on the run and getting rid of dead bodies.

Bryce finally knocked on the bathroom door, letting us know it was okay to come out. I felt relief tingling through my body. I exhaled in a show of relief. I heard Lamar do the same thing.

"That shit worked like a charm. The cop thought we was up in here fucking all day long, so he assumed that we ain't see no housekeeper," Bryce said proudly, amused that his plan had worked.

I found that the strangest shit amused that crazy-ass nigga. Cora was still laying in the bed. That bitch was probably too afraid to move until somebody told her to move.

"That was good thinking. C'mon, Cora, get up and get dressed. We gettin' the fuck up outta here as soon as the police get out of the motel," Lamar announced to all of us.

Cora got out of the bed and quickly put her clothes on.

We all sat around in silence for about thirty minutes. Once in a while somebody would say a word or two, but for the most part, we were all drained and didn't have shit to say to each other.

The sky outside finally got dark enough to move the body without really worrying about a lot of people being around. But we still had to wait a few minutes for the cops to finish their search of the other rooms. We knew there were only a few more rooms left for them to go in that dank little-ass motel.

I couldn't help but to keep eyeing the telephone wire that was lying on the floor. We had used it to tie up the dead housekeeper at first, and then Bryce and Lamar used to later to tie Cora up. I looked down at the wire, and my mind started racing like the internal hard drive of a computer. I was processing information a mile a minute all while I was scheming long and hard. A chick like me had come up with a quick plan. It was a now-or-never, but I was willing to try anything.

I was planning to plug that wire back into the phone as soon as Lamar and Bryce stepped out of that room. I knew from the last time I'd tried to use it that the phone only called the front desk. But I was going to have the front desk assist me in making a collect call to my family or to Mario. I was fucking desperate after all of this mayhem. I wasn't trying to go back on the road with Bryce and Lamar. They had gotten me into enough extra trouble for a lifetime.

As my mind was racing with ways to get away, I looked Cora's body up and down and decided that I would be able to take her down if she tried to jump bad when I tried to make my phone calls.

Yoshi, this is the only opportunity you're going to have to get the fuck away from here, I told myself. I didn't know where I would go, but I was going to plug in that phone, get a collect call to my cousin, and get the fuck out of there. I would go into hiding until my cousin could drive the few hours from Virginia up to Delaware and get me.

It sounded all good to me as I repeated the plan to myself, but of course, with my luck, who knew what would actually go down? I had to try, though.

Bryce and Lamar got ready to move the body. And I got ready to make my move.

SECOND NATURE

Just as I suspected, Bryce and Lamar instructed me and Cora to stay in the room until they were able to stuff the housekeeper into the trunk of the car. At first it looked like they would just leave us alone. I got excited thinking I could execute my plan with the telephone easily. But Lamar must've had ESP because he walked over to the motel phone, unplugged the receiver, picked up the wire off the floor, and took them with him.

As I watched him, I was so mad, I could've slapped his ass. He evidently knew how my mind worked, and he also knew I wasn't a fucking dummy like his little girlfriend. I guess Lamar wasn't trying to let me get one phone call off because he knew I would be calling somebody and telling them what was going on. He gave me a snide look as he took the phone pieces, and he and Bryce left the room.

I sat on the bed while Cora got up and watched Lamar and Bryce from the window. I was so mad, I felt like killing her ass too. While she was preoccupied watching the guys, I scanned the room for a sharp object to use as my personal weapon just in case Bryce got any crazy ideas after the body of the housekeeper was in the car. It was no secret that he wanted me eliminated, so I knew I needed something to defend myself with if we were going back on the road.

But my search was to no avail. I didn't find anything. There wasn't a goddamn thing in that room I could fashion into a weapon. All I could do was shake my head in disgust and bury my face in the palm of my hands.

Moments later I heard Cora pull the curtain back to cover the window, and then she took two steps back. Even though I wasn't looking at her, I could tell that she stood still. My face was still buried in my hands, but I felt a strong urge to look up. Something inside of me told me she was staring at me. So when I looked up and saw that's what she was doing, I damn near screamed.

"Why the fuck are you staring at me?" I had really had enough of that bitch.

"Because I can," she replied.

Oh, this bitch wanted to get bold because Lamar and Bryce weren't around. I wasn't in the fucking mood for her at all. The way I felt, I could've torn her the fuck apart with my bare hands.

"Well, I don't know why your dumb ass is looking at me, because if you wouldn't have come here then none of this shit would've happened."

She gave me a snide look and said, "Bitch, I came here because I wanted to. I've got a whole lot to say to you, Yoshi."

"Don't you think you've said and done enough? You're the reason why the poor lady is dead, and all you can do is stand up there looking like a big-ass goofball while they put her body in the trunk of a fuckin' car like a piece of trash? You should be the one in the trunk of that car." I had been calm for a while, but after I realized the phone call wouldn't happen, I just let it all hang out on that bitch.

"Fuck you, bitch!" she screamed, and then she lunged at me with her right hand in midair and her fist balled. She was only a couple feet away from me.

I jumped to my feet and waited for her to come close enough, so I could prevent her from hammering me on top of my head, seeing that I was sitting low on the bed and she was standing up. My first thought was to trip her with my feet, but instead I reached behind me, snatched the telephone base, and bashed her across the face with it.

Caught off guard by the blow to her head, Cora stumbled backwards and collapsed onto the floor. I guess I had rehashed her old injuries from Lamar's previous beating because she looked like she was in a hell of a lot of pain.

The moment she hit the floor, I dropped the phone and rushed over and locked the door. When I looked back at Cora, I saw her trying to get up from the floor, so I rushed toward her and started stomping her and kicking her in the side. She screamed really loud, which of course got the attention of Lamar and Bryce outside.

I heard them struggling to get back into the room. I heard Lamar yell lightly through the door and ask me to open it. I could tell his face was up close to the door. He was probably in a frenzy because he was out there in disguise. I panicked because I knew if I didn't open the door, they would bust it open, drawing a lot of attention, and that would be my ass.

That's all I needed—fucking crazy Bryce breathing up my asshole.

My heart started racing out of control. I rushed into the bathroom and lock the door behind me. After all of these days and at that moment, I could finally picture Mario's face. I started wishing he was around or that I could at least speak to him. I wanted so desperately to let him know that I was all right and that I had nothing to do with the U.S. Marshals getting murdered. I also wanted him to contact my family and the police. But, again, I wasn't able to do that, because there was no connection or wires in the phone line.

While I frantically tried to think about what to do next, I noticed that Lamar and Bryce had finally gotten the door open. And even though they were seconds away from grabbing a hold of me, I continued to try to get away. The window in the bathroom was small, but I figured if I maneuvered my body in the right direction I would be able to get through it. So I climbed into the bathtub and stood on the ledge.

"She's trying to climb out the bathroom window!" Bryce panicked and rushed over toward me.

Lamar slammed the door shut and raced toward me too. The only thing I could think of doing was to scream. After all of these days I was at the end of my rope. I screamed, "Help!" as loudly as I possibly could out of the bathroom window. I didn't care who heard me.

But my cry for help was abruptly cut off when Lamar snatched me down from the window and Bryce backhanded me across my face. The blunt force knocked me back into the tub. The impact of his knuckles stung my face severely, and all I could do was press my left hand against that side of my cheek. I just gave up. I was in the death bathroom anyway.

Meanwhile, as I lay my back against the cold ceramic tiles of the bathroom wall, Bryce and Lamar both stood over top of me like they were about to kill me.

Lamar spoke up first. "Come on now, Yoshi. Why did you do that? You know Bryce is about two seconds from filling you up with gunpowder."

Bryce eyed me evilly. "I told you we should've done that bitch in a long time ago. Do you see that she is becoming a bigger problem than what we started with?"

Lamar took his eyes off me and looked directly at Bryce. "You gotta focus, Bryce."

"I am focused!" Bryce snapped. "You gotta stop actin' like a bitch-ass nigga when it comes to these two bitches."

Lamar didn't answer. He just grabbed me out of the tub.

Cora finally pulled herself together and was able to get up from the floor. The right side of her face turned even more black and blue than before. I really hit her smack dab over her right eye, and it was ugly. She sat down on the chair placed at the motel door and started whining about the pain in her face. Lamar and Bryce both ignored her and kept their attention on me.

"Why you wait until a time like this to try to escape, Yoshi?" Lamar asked me. This nigga was acting like I had hurt his feelings on something.

"Now this bitch just probably brought mad attention to this fuckin' room. I swear, I'm not going down for none of y'all muthafuckas. I will smoke all of you bitches up in here first." Bryce said.

Lamar shook his head like he was utterly disgusted with me. I knew that whatever he was thinking wasn't anything good. The likelihood that he would fight to keep Bryce from doing me in didn't look good either. The best thing for me to do was pray.

I immediately closed my eyes to block out everyone around me, but that was quickly interrupted when Bryce grabbed me around my throat and began to choke the hell out of me again. I knew exactly what he was capable of from our last incident, so I immediately went into defense mode to fight him off. Shit, I had no idea if Lamar would save me again.

"I oughta kill your ass now, bitch!" Bryce said, grinding his teeth.

Lamar grabbed a hold of Bryce's arms and yanked them from my neck as hard as he could. "Yo, Bryce, enough, man! We gotta get the fuck out of here before the motel manager calls the police."

Cora sat back on the chair rubbing her head and said, "He probably already has."

"Yeah, that's why we should be getting the fuck out of here right now," Lamar replied.

He grabbed me by the arm roughly and led me toward the door. He wasn't going to take another chance with me acting stupid again.

Bryce did the same with Cora. I saw her crinkle up her face because his hands were much bigger than Lamar's. I was sure he was hurting her ass as he dragged her along. I guess Bryce and Lamar were tired of me and Cora's asses. We had put them at risk in more ways than one, so it was obvious they weren't going to take another chance on either one of us fucking up this whole escape plan.

With the men holding onto us, we finally headed out of the motel room. As soon as we started walking, we heard someone screaming out and running toward us.

I could see that it was a man, but I didn't know exactly who it was until he got closer. As soon as he got a little closer, we all seemed to notice him at the same damn time. It was the motel manager. All of us were stuck on stupid because the man was absolutely frantic, waving his arms and yelling out to us.

"What this nigga want now?" Lamar grumbled, digging his thumb and forefinger deeper into my arm.

"See I fuckin' told you, nigga. This bitch done called attention to us," Bryce gritted.

"Hey! Hey! Wait a minute!" the manager was calling out, running at us like we were leaving without paying or something.

"Fuck, fuck, fuck!" Bryce gritted some more. He gave me the evil eye. I could feel the heat from his eyes burning on me.

The motel manager was finally up on us, and he was breathing hard from running. Bryce just stood very still as he watched the man.

"Can we help you?" Lamar asked nervously.

"Somebody was yelling for help from this room. What is going on here?" the motel manager asked, looking from face to face.

I guess he noticed Cora's bruises, my wild hair, and saw Bryce and Lamar holding onto us and thought we were being beat up or something. Plus, I knew then that he had heard me screaming out of the bathroom window like I didn't have any sense. I wanted to ask the old man to call the cops so bad, but instead, and once again, I just remained quiet, following Bryce and Lamar's lead.

Bryce stepped up to the old man in a menacing way. He was like a giant compared to the skinny, little, frail old man. The old man looked like he had to break his neck to look up at Bryce.

"I just wanted to know if the girls over here were all right. I heard somebody screaming out of this room. A lady is missing around here, and I'm just on edge," the old man explained.

"Yo, old man, mind ya fuckin' business," Bryce gritted. "We got everything here under control."

Bryce just couldn't be nice to save his life. The old man kept looking from face to face, his hands shaking after Bryce barked on him. I swear I kind of felt a little sorry for the poor little man.

"I-I just"—The motel manager cut his own words short and started staring at me and Lamar real, real hard.

I knew right away that this man had recognized us from the news reports. His eyes seemed to grow wider in size by the second. The old man abruptly turned around and started walking back toward the motel lobby area where his desk was.

Lamar let my arm go and looked like he was going to chase after the man, but he didn't.

"Yo, Bryce, this muthafucka recognized me and Yoshi. He gotta go. This nigga gotta die. He's probably on his way to call the cops. I'm sure this car is on the surveillance camera, and he got a picture of you on that ID. He gotta go, young. Hurry up and do what you gotta do, so we can get the fuck up outta here," Lamar told Bryce.

Bryce pulled his burner from his waistband and rushed after the old man. The old man kept walking fast and looking back, fear showing in his eyes. When the man looked back and saw Bryce coming after him, he tried to run, but he was way too slow for Bryce's big, long-legged strides coming behind him. Bryce caught up to him in no time.

"Please!" the old man begged, after noticing the gun in Bryce's hand.

When Bryce was close enough, he let off one shot that hit the man right in the back of the head.

I jumped fiercely at the sound of the gunshot and watched as the old man's body thrust forward and fell to the ground. "Oh my God! I can't believe somebody else had to die because of all of this bullshit!" I cried out angrily.

I was so through with all of this death and killing going on just because this nigga wanted to escape. There was a full fucking manhunt going on for us right now, and these niggas were still killing fucking people. I just kept shaking my head from side to side.

"Lamar, stop all this killing, please," I begged him.

"This time it was your dumb-ass fault," Cora made a point to say.

"Shut the fuck up, bitch! I'm warning you," I replied, pointing my finger at her. I was one second from attacking that bitch again.

Lamar lost it. "Both of y'all need to shut the fuck up! Y'all both been doin' dumb shit, and y'all both have caused me unnecessary fuckin' stress. Now shut the fuck up!" Then he roughly forced me into the backseat of the car.

"Cora, you drive the car you came in and follow us out of here. Don't try no funny shit until I tell you, you can go the fuck back to D.C. Now get the fuck in the car!" Lamar barked.

I could tell he was frustrated and had had enough. He was kind of coming apart at the seams because the cool, calm, and collected Lamar was changing.

Bryce came rushing back toward the car. He jumped into the driver's seat and screeched the car to the front of the motel. I couldn't for the life of me understand why he would be fucking stopping to go inside the motel office when he had just killed the manager and, plus, he still had a fucking body in the trunk of the car.

"What the fuck is he doing?" I asked Lamar.

"He is going to get the surveillance tapes and get the ID copies with his pictures on it," Lamar explained nervously.

It made sense, but it had me on edge still. "Well, shit, he might was well leave the lady's body here too. We done made this motel a fuckin' crime scene anyway. One more dead body next to that old man ain't gonna make no difference. Why chance it on the road with a body in the trunk?"

It was not like I was purposely giving them sinister ideas on how to cover up murders, but it just made sense. If we got pulled over on the highway, having a body in the trunk wouldn't be a good look, especially if it got to a point where a cop called in those cadaver dogs.

The idea must've seemed like a good one to Lamar, because as

Bryce was inside getting rid of evidence, Lamar rushed out of the car, opened the trunk, and dumped the housekeeper's body right fucking there.

A few seconds later, Bryce and Lamar jumped back into the car at the same time, and we skidded the fuck out of there. It was a good thing not too many people patronized that run-down motel, or else we would have had witnesses galore. I had scanned the area several times, and I didn't notice one person outside looking at us. So as far as myself, Lamar, and Bryce were concerned, we were all in the free and clear.

BLINDED

I was sitting in the back of that car with so much shit on my mind. I was mentally and physically exhausted. I lay my head back on the seat as we drove away from Delaware. I closed my eyes, and sleep momentarily overcame me.

Then all of a sudden, I felt the car come to a stop. I was leery anytime we came to sudden stops. I always thought it was either the cops getting us or that Lamar and Bryce were about to off my ass and throw me in a ditch somewhere.

I opened my eyes to look out the window, and it was dark as shit outside. It was scary as hell too. I balled my fists up in defense. I was getting myself ready. If either Bryce or Lamar tried to drag me out of the car, I was planning to fight for my life like never before. In other words, I was ready to swing on either one of those muthafuckas.

We had pulled off the highway on a desolate exit and down an even more desolate-looking road. I saw Lamar get out, and I followed him with my eyes. That's when I noticed Cora had pulled up behind us in the car she was driving. She had gotten out of her car too.

Lamar went up to her and hugged her. I wasn't jealous, just confused. I guess he wanted to send her back to D.C. on a good note, so she wouldn't snitch on him.

"This nigga here actin' all lovey-dovey," Bryce complained out loud.

I kind of agreed with Bryce on that note. I just couldn't understand it either. I mean, here we were on the run, and Lamar was stopping to give this bitch a hug after she fucked him over.

I couldn't hear what Cora and Lamar were saying to each other, but judging from the way she was holding onto him like she would never see him again, it seemed like they were saying their good-byes. I still couldn't believe that he'd allowed her to hug him after all she had done to get us into this situation in the first place.

Bryce was complaining the entire time, talking to himself, saying shit like Lamar should have let him kill Cora and Lamar is a soft nigga for love. I wanted to tell Bryce that some people did have feelings, and not everyone was like his cold, calculating, psychopath ass. Instead, I stayed silent and I kept watching Lamar and Cora have their moment.

All of a sudden, Lamar stopped hugging Cora, and he bent into her and gave her a deep tongue-kiss. I scrunched up my face, watching them intently. Lamar was saying something to her. I noticed her wiping tears from her face. Maybe he was telling her he would never see her again or some shit like that.

Cora turned around and started to walk back to her car, and Lamar just stood there watching her for a few seconds. Then I noticed Lamar hesitate for a minute, like he was about to walk back to the car I was in so we could head out. But he didn't.

My eyes popped open as I watched him go into his waistband and pull out a gun. I opened my eyes even fucking wider as he rushed up behind Cora. He yelled out something to her, but I couldn't hear him because Bryce had the music up loud in the car. Cora turned around slightly, and before she knew what hit her, Lamar shot her in her head. I saw blood spray onto her car from the gunshot wound in her head, and her body dropped to the ground like a ton of bricks.

Lamar didn't even stand around and look. He just turned right around, ran back to the car, and jumped in. He was breathing so hard, I could hear every breath he took, and I was all the way in the backseat. Before he could even fully close the door, Bryce peeled out.

Lamar had left Cora's car running, and her body on the ground outside of it. These niggas were ruthless as hell, leaving bodies piled up everywhere we went. If Lamar killed a bitch like Cora that he cared about, shit, I really needed to be worried for my safety. At that point, I had no more hope of making it back to Miami in one piece. I couldn't even think of one fucking reason Bryce and Lamar would keep me alive. Not only was I still a liability as a high-profile escaped prisoner, but now I had witnessed them commit a handful of murders with no remorse or regard for human life at all.

"Yo, *L*, you seem all down and shit. You ain't have no choice after what that bitch put you through," Bryce told Lamar. "You need to smoke some of that kush and get ya mind right, nigga. You on your way to full freedom."

Lamar said to Bryce, "I'm just having second thoughts about everything. What if that connect up top act up and shit? I mean, it ain't no guarantee I can even use the fuckin' fake passport to get out, you know what I'm sayin'?"

I was listening to Lamar's every word, but I was acting like I had fallen asleep.

"All of this bullshit with these bitches and loss of life may be for fuckin' nothing in the end," he added.

Lamar was pouring out his feelings, but I still didn't know what to believe about him. I had seen so many sides of him—sensitive; protective; angry; sweet; and now murderous. It was just all so confusing.

After we drove for about another hour or so, I looked up at a sign on the highway and saw that we were about to get onto the New Jersey Turnpike, heading north. That was kind of alarming to me. I couldn't figure out why they would be heading to either New York or New Jersey, where cops would be swarming everywhere because of the crime rates. Plus, I was one hundred percent sure that our pictures were flying around those cities.

I wanted to ask them where exactly we were going, but I knew after my last stunt, neither Bryce or Lamar trusted me enough to tell me jack shit about our future whereabouts. So once again, Yoshi Lomax remained silent and let fate take over her life and lead her down some unknown path.

The whole time we were driving, I was thinking and rethinking about how I could get the fuck away from them. The first time I wasn't well prepared to make a run for it, and that bitch Cora was a big hindrance to me. But this time I promised myself, if I tried to escape again, I would think shit through and do it right.

"Yo, I can't wait to get to New York and offload this bitch," Bryce said. He turned around quickly to see me playing possum.

"Ain't nothing going to change when we get there. I'm still going to tell you the same shit—Leave Yoshi alone," Lamar said, taking up for me as usual. "Let me get your phone. I wanna make sure shit is all set when we get there so I don't have to stay long, even though a nigga can get lost forever in the city that never sleeps."

Bryce handed Lamar his cell phone. Lamar dialed some numbers, and then that nigga started speaking French again. That same disturbing feeling came over me again, and I shifted uncomfortably in the backseat. I couldn't understand anything he was saying on the phone, but I was well aware that New York had a huge population of Haitians. I wanted to shit my pants.

Then the more I thought about it, I concluded to myself that the probability of Bryce and Lamar knowing Sheldon Chisolm had to be low. As I thought about how crazy it sounded, I scolded myself for having such dumb thoughts. Shit, if it turned out that Lamar and Bryce were Haitian, it still didn't mean they would know a Haitian from Miami. I was definitely being paranoid.

I opened my eyes to see exactly where we were, and when we passed the New York City sign, my heart jerked in my chest. The prospect of getting lost in that big-ass city were great. I had been back to New York a few times when I was still practicing law and was familiar with some places. I was thinking, if I could only get away from them, since New York was one of the very few places that still had pay telephones, I would be able to reach out to Mario. I also knew that with a good disguise anybody could get totally lost in the crowds of New York. It would be possible to walk right past a million people and only two may recognize me, if that.

By the time we reached Brooklyn, it was one o'clock in the morning according to the clock on the dashboard. I sat up in the seat and looked out of the window to take in all of the scenery. There were a lot of people still outside on the street, even though it was late.

Lamar and Bryce were trying to figure out the directions to their destination, so we made a bunch of twists and turns and ups and downs. Finally, after they argued for a few minutes and got themselves together, we pulled up to Fulton Street. There were a bunch of silver gates pulled down, like there were closed stores up and down the street. There was a Kentucky Fried Chicken on the corner. It was one of the things I noted as I tried to make mental notes of the landmarks that would be easy to remember.

I looked over at the cross street sign, and it said Nostrand Avenue. I put those streets in my head and committed them to memory. Even though it was one in the morning, it really stood out in my mind that there were so many people outside. New York really was the city that never slept. I had no idea what type of adventure these two were taking me on this time, but I braced myself for the worst.

"Yo, get the fuck up, troublemaker," Bryce called out to me.

I guess his dumb ass hadn't noticed that I had been up surveying the area for an escape route. "I'm already up," I said with attitude.

"We gettin' ready to get out and go into that building," Bryce said. "If you make any sudden moves, you gon' end up just like the rest of the people we left behind at the motel."

I took his warning and digested it for sure.

"A'ight, get the money out," Lamar told Bryce.

There was a long, awkward pause.

Lamar asked Bryce for the money again. Bryce cleared his throat over and over again.

"Yo, man, I didn't get the chance to tell you, with all the drama shit that was going on, something went wrong with the fuckin' loot." Then he did that stupid throat-clearing thing again and again.

"What! You had the whole fuckin' ride here to tell me! What went wrong? How much do you have?" Lamar screamed.

Bryce didn't answer; just more throat-clearing.

"Don't tell me you don't have any of it!" Lamar barked, slamming his fists on the dashboard.

Damn. I thought he would break the damn dashboard, as hard as he was hitting it.

"I tried to do all I could do. I couldn't get the money from the drops. Niggas wasn't trying to come up off what they promised because they didn't believe me that you were using it to buy a way out of the country. Niggas took advantage of you not being around. I'm telling you the truth, *L.* Don't worry about it. We gon' have to see if the connect up here will make a deal and shit."

"These are fuckin' gangstas—Ain't no let's-make-a-deal bullshit flying with them," Lamar explained.

I could tell by the high pitch in Lamar's voice he was now stressed the fuck out.

"Let's just go up there and talk to dude," Bryce told Lamar, trying to comfort him. "You never know."

"You better hope this nigga still wants to hook me up with a way out of here, or else all this shit would be for fuckin' nothing. I don't know what's gon' happen with us if I can't get the fuck out of Dodge. I guess we all goin' down in that case."

I could tell Lamar wasn't really feeling Bryce right then. That could worked in my favor, so I made a mental note of that too.

"Let's go, Yoshi. When we get upstairs, don't say a fuckin' word either," Lamar told me.

We all got out of the car and walked up to a door. The door looked hidden amongst all of the store gates. It was also beat-down like it had been hit with a sledgehammer and maybe even a few bullets.

I crinkled up my face in part confusion and part disgust. Here I was, the once great Yoshi Lomax, in the hood about to run up in a spot against my will, and where I had no idea what was going on inside.

Bryce did some crazy-ass knock, and we were allowed inside. When I stepped across the doorway, the odors inside threatened to make me throw up. It was like a mixture of stale weed smoke, ass, and some sort of cologne or perfume. Whatever it was, the combination was lethal to the nostrils.

I put my forearm over my nose to try to keep from smelling that shit. Lamar rushed up a flight of stairs that was right in front of us, and me and Bryce followed him. Those stairs were so rickety, it felt like I could fall through them at any minute.

"What kind of place is this?" I finally asked. Fuck being quiet, I wanted to know where the hell we were going.

"Just keep fuckin' walking, troublemaker," Bryce gritted.

I stomped up the steps after that. When we got to the top of the landing, Lamar led us into an apartment. It was definitely where all the weed smoke was coming from. Shit, I felt like I could get high off the smell of the weed alone.

"Stay out here with Yoshi," Lamar told Bryce.

Bryce didn't seem like he was too happy with the idea, and neither was I.

Lamar wasn't gone long before he came rushing back out of the apartment. He was whispering, and I was stretching my ears to listen.

"He showed me the passport, and all of the papers look legit as hell. He told me his brother and a few street muthafuckas got out of the country with the shit he got because he got a hookup inside the State Department."

"Well, that's good then," Bryce said.

"Nah, you don't understand. This nigga said no money, no deal, unless we have something else to offer," Lamar whispered to Bryce.

I could hear every word he was saying.

If he didn't have any money, what else would he offer him?

"The thing is," Lamar said, "you know what he does and the kind of different operations he has, right? So now I'm right here, and I got a good match to one of his main markets, you feel me?"

Bryce was nodding his head in the affirmative, and all I could do was continue to eavesdrop, confused as hell.

"I told him it was a rare find, you know, the mixture we got, right. So the nigga said it's better than money, so right now we need to move it so he can see it," Lamar said, continuing to speak in code.

"I got you," Bryce said. Then he just turned toward me. Then he grabbed me up like I was a piece of property and started carrying me into the apartment.

"Get off of me!" I screamed out. "I can fuckin' walk! What are you doing?" I started kicking and punching Bryce in his gorilla back as I hung over one of his huge shoulders. Oh my God, I was in a state of shock right then. *How could this be happening?* "Lamar! Help me! Lamar!" I called out. I could feel the blood rushing to my head as I flailed and kicked and screamed for dear life.

Lamar didn't say a fucking word. He just kept following behind Bryce as he carried me. I knew the days of Lamar always taking up for me would come to an end sooner or later.

Bryce carried me down a long-ass hallway, and the whole time I continued to try to fight. All of my efforts were for nothing, though. I was no match for Bryce.

We finally went into a dimly lit room at the end of the hallway. From Bryce's shoulders I could see women posted up all over the room, some sitting, some standing, and they were all in different stages of undress.

"Lamar, what the fuck it this?" I hollered.

Some of the women looked at me, others seemed like they were too spaced-out to even notice me.

Bryce finally lowered me from his shoulders onto the floor. "Don't fuckin' try to run," he hissed in my ear. "If you know like I know, you will just stand still and be fuckin' quiet."

His breath smelled just like a pile of horseshit, and it was making me nauseous. I kept looking around and around, my mind racing with a billion crazy thoughts. Lamar was standing there like a statue, not saying a word. Then another door opened, and three men came out. I could tell the one in the middle was some kind of boss because, the way the other two flanked him, they were obviously his bodyguards or some sort of security.

"Here she is, just like I promised," Lamar said to the man.

"What! What the fuck are you talking about, Lamar?" I screamed.

Bryce then put his hands on my shoulders and squeezed them so hard, I almost dropped to my knees. "I told you to shut the fuck up and stand still," he said, bearing down into my skin unmercifully.

"She is half-Korean and half-Black. Like I told you, she is gon' be real good for your business. You can use her to get to a different market and shit," Lamar told the man.

I was flabbergasted. This muthafucka Lamar was selling me into what looked like some sort of human trafficking or prostitution ring.

The man stepped closer to me, and I shrank back from his grill. He wore a black eye patch, and one side of his face was completely disfigured, like he had been burned with acid or something. He didn't have much hair on that side either, just little sprouts that grew there sparsely.

"She look nice. Nice legs, long hair, pretty skin. I like her," the man said with an Asian accent I didn't recognize at first. He reached out to touch my face, and I immediately noticed how long and nasty his nails were.

I turned my face away as tears slid down my cheeks. I wanted to run, but it was like my feet were planted in cement and stuck there.

"See, like I told you she is better than any money I could pay you," Lamar said, selling me to the man like I was a piece of meat.

I had to wonder if this was why he kept me alive all of this time—as fucking collateral.

"Okay, we have a deal," the man said.

When he said that, something inside of me snapped. I didn't know if it was the finality of it all or if it was just my natural-born instincts to survive, but I lifted my foot and kicked that muthafucka in his balls, hard. I was surprised by my own strength. Then I stepped on Bryce's foot and whirled around and started running top speed to the door. I made it out into that long hallway and started hauling ass like my life depended on it. I could tell someone was chasing me, and without looking back, I instinctively knew it was Lamar. We both had a lot to lose at this point. He needed me to get his fake passport and ID and a way out of the country, and I needed to get the fuck out of there.

I was finally at the steps, and I started going down them almost two by two. Then I heard a shot. I felt like a bullet whizzed past my face. I got to the downstairs door, but it was all bolted up from the inside.

"Noooo!" I screamed out as I started pulling on the door. There were about forty locks on, all kinds of dead bolts and shit. I finally turned around and just fell down on the floor crying.

Lamar was over me in no time. He grabbed me at the top of my head by my hair. "Get the fuck up!" he growled.

I looked up into his face and didn't even recognize him. He seemed like a totally different person than the one I knew all of this time. He dragged me back up the stairs and back down that ominous hallway.

Once we were back in the room, I noticed that the scary, nasty man was sitting down on a huge reclining chair.

"She very feisty, huh?" the man asked Lamar.

He was Asian—I assumed Chinese because I would've recognized a Korean accent.

"I'm sorry," Lamar said. "That shit won't happen again. She was just losing her fuckin' mind for a minute."

"I don't need no problem. If she a problem, she no good for my business," the man said.

"No, no. She's good. She don't have a choice. This is my payment for my shit. I gotta get out of here," Lamar said, sounding like a desperate fucking wimp.

I had lost all respect that I had for Lamar. If I could've just put my hands around his throat, I would've squeezed him until all of the life left his body. I hated him and everything he stood for.

"Make her strip. I need to see body," the man said.

I started flailing and kicking again. Fuck that! I wasn't going down without a fight. "I'm not fuckin' taking off my clothes for nobody!" I screamed at the top of my lungs. "I fuckin' cannot believe you, Lamar! You bastard! Why didn't you just let me go back to Miami and go back to prison? You fuckin' traitor! Karma will catch up to you!"

Out of the corner of my eye, I saw Bryce coming toward me. I knew whatever was going to happen next wasn't going to be good.

"Shut the fuck up and take your fuckin' clothes off!" Bryce gritted, getting up in my face in a menacing way.

"Fuck you!" I screamed, and I spat right in his fucking face.

Bryce wiped the spit from his face and looked at me. His eyeballs seemed as if they had turned red, he was so mad.

"I'm not strippi—"

My words were cut short when I suddenly felt a sharp pain in the back of my head. Somebody had definitely hit me, I was sure. Next, the room started closing in around me, and my ears were ringing. I had been knocked to the floor. That much I knew because, although my eyes were kind of out of focus, I remember landing on the floor with a loud thud.

Then darkness overcame me. All sight and sound had ceased for me. I had definitely been knocked the fuck out, because I don't remember a goddamn thing after that. I was laid the fuck out and not aware of what would happen next.

WHAT THE FUCK
JUST HAPPENED?

When I opened my eyes, the pain that shot through the back of my head was crazy. "Oww!" I winced, trying to get my eyes to focus on my surroundings.

I started moving my arms and legs, and that's when I noticed I was being touched all over my body by what felt like a bunch of little hands. "What the fuck!" I screamed out, trying to jump up. But when I did that, the pain in my head intensified, and I was kind of forced to relax my ass back down on that bed. I continued to feel the touching. It was more like rubbing or something.

"Hello," I heard a soft voice say to me.

I moved my head and looked to my left and then my right. I was surrounded by about two little Asian women. They were soft-spoken, and they were also undressing me.

"What are y'all doing to me?" I cried out as I tried to pull my arms and legs away from them.

"We help you take a bath. Change dirty clothes. Get clean up," one of the Asian women said to me.

I couldn't even front. Although I was in a fucked-up position right now, that woman's voice was soothing to me. The women weren't aggressive or mean at all, and they also looked like they wouldn't harm a fly, because they were so small. If I wasn't so weak and in so much pain, I probably would have gotten up and tried to make a run for it.

After a while, I finally stopped trying to keep them from undressing me, and I let them get me out of those dirty, disgusting clothes I had been wearing for days. Two of the women helped me sit up and get off the bed. When I looked around at the place we were in, I was in awe. It was nothing like the little hole-in-the-wall place Lamar and Bryce had dropped me off at. The house we were in was nice and upscale with expensive, ultramodern furniture, and artwork on the walls. It reminded me of my posh condo I had left behind in Miami.

"Where are we?" I asked.

Neither one of the women answered.

"You take bath now," one of them said.

They led me into the bathroom, where there was a huge luxurious bathtub in the center of the floor and the walls were covered in glass tiles. I looked over at the bath, and there were piles of rose petals floating in the water. The bath looked so inviting, I felt like I was floating over to it.

"Flower soothe tired skin. Make repair to bruises," one of the little ladies said to me.

I looked down at my body, particularly my arms and legs. Sure enough, my arms and legs were covered in small bruises. I guess I got those bruises while I was fighting Bryce and Lamar to escape from that man. The memory of exactly what had happened to me was still fuzzy in my mind. It hurt my brain to even try to remember.

Those nice little women helped me move gently. I was led to the tub, and they helped me get into the water. I inhaled deeply because the water was so damn hot, but it was also soothing as hell. I exhaled and sat back against a bath pillow that they had set inside the tub.

"Enjoy . . . few minutes," one of the ladies said.

The other lady sat in a small chair and just watched me. She made me feel uncomfortable, so I closed my eyes and just imagined that I was back in Miami in my old condo, with my old life. I pictured Mario, and I thought about Grandma Hattie and my cousins. It was a false sense of security, though.

After about fifteen minutes, the other woman came back into the bathroom. "You need to wash good. Shave all places. Clean your nail and hair. Be perfect," the lady said to me.

I was thinking, *How is this bitch going to tell me I have to shave and shit? What business is it of hers whether or not I shave?*

The woman handed me some lavender-scented soap, a razor, and some sweet-smelling shampoo. Ultimately I did as I was told. I washed my skin over and over again because it felt so good not to be in one of those grungy-ass motel showers anymore.

"You hurry," the other woman who had been watching me said.

They were getting on my fucking nerves. I mean, even though they spoke softly and were fairly nice, they seemed nervous and were rushing for some strange reason.

When I was done cleaning myself up, I stood up, and both women ran to the side of the tub and helped me get out. I swear, it was like they thought I was a precious commodity that they were afraid to break or something. They led me back into the room where the bed was. They had a beautiful Carolina Herrera dress laid out on the bed and jewelry next to it, and a pair of beautiful Dolce &

Gabbana pumps on the floor.

"You wear this. Boss say so," one of the ladies said to me.

At first I was more than happy to be putting on some of the fancy items I was used to wearing in my past. But I had to become suspicious as to why I would be dressed up so nicely. I had no clue what kind of shit these people were into.

"Where are we going?" I asked.

Of course, neither one of these bitches wanted to answer the question. They just started holding out shit for me to put on—La Perla thong and bra, La Mer lotion, and then the dress, jewelry, and shoes. Next, they walked me over to a vanity chair, and one of them started brushing out my hair. She took my hair and pulled it up onto my head in an haute couture-style bun. They worked together to apply my makeup.

Don't ask me why I just sat there and let these women dress me up when I surely could have fucked them both up and made a run for it. But I went along with it all, and truthfully, I felt damn good about myself when they were finally finished and I was allowed to view the final product. My head still hurt a little bit, but my self-esteem was back intact after I whirled around and looked at myself over and over again in the mirror. I hadn't been dressed up like that in a long time. There were no luxury amenities in prison, and there damn sure weren't any while I was on the run with Lamar and Bryce. I had to smile at the vision of myself in the mirror. But that little streak of joy was short-lived.

"We must go now," one of the women called out to me. She was the one who seemed like the head bitch in charge. She was older, and I noticed she was slightly more demanding than the other woman. She was calling all the shots and constantly updating someone on her cell phone. She spoke in Cantonese, so I couldn't understand her. Damn, how I wished she was Korean so I could understand her. I was eyeing that fucking cell phone. That was what I needed to get my hands on.

As I was being led out of the huge house, I noticed all of the armed guards around. They seemed to be everywhere. I couldn't figure out why the hell they were there. I immediately felt deflated because I was sure I would be able to take the two little bitches down and get the fuck out of there. We stood at the front of the big house, and I saw a line of women just as pretty or even prettier than me. They were all dressed similar to me in expensive dresses and jewelry.

We were loaded into different vehicles. I was put into a black Lincoln Town Car, and the two women came into the car with me. I guess they were assigned to handle me. We drove for a long time. I could tell we were in Manhattan because I noticed the Empire State Building in the distance. The house we were in before we started driving must've been in Long Island or far out of the city.

We finally drove into an underground garage and parked. The two women helped me get out of the car. They were busying themselves fixing my dress, my hair, and my makeup. It was like they wanted to make sure I looked perfect with not a hair out of place. Finally, we all walked into a door, and that's when shit got crazy.

"I need put this on you eyes," the head woman said. Then she placed a black scarf over my eyes so I couldn't see shit. They started leading me to wherever we were going. We finally came to a stop, and I could sense that I was in a room full of people. There were different scents of colognes and perfumes, and I could hear the murmur of voices. When the blindfold was removed from my eyes, I realized I was surrounded by some of the same women I had seen back at the house. A lot of them were Asian or white, like Russian or something. I seemed to be the only one with any trace of black heritage.

None of the other women spoke a word. It was like they already knew what was going to happen next. My two handlers left me in the room. The next thing I knew, me and all of the women were herded onto some type of stage by some of the armed men and examined there.

"Put out your hands," a tall Chinese man told me.

I put out my hands, and he looked at my nails and under them. He did that to all of the women.

"Line up . . . straight line," the man called out, and we all did as we were told.

Then I noticed more armed guards posted up everywhere, so any thought of making a run for it again was dead for me. But that was just for the time being. I was always scheming up a way to get away.

We were all lined up on a stage with bright lights shining down on us, and I could feel the heat from the lights on my face. I looked out into the crowd and saw nothing but men sitting down and filing into the room. It was crazy to me. The men coming into the room were almost all Asian, with a few white faces and a couple of black faces in the crowd, all dressed in suits and ties. It looked just like some sort of business convention. I looked up and down the line of women. We all looked like we were about to parade ourselves in a beauty pageant.

"Good evening," a man's voice boomed through a speaker system, and all of the men hurried to take their seats and directed their attention to the front.

Suddenly someone grabbed me from the back and whispered, "Keep your face straight, stand up tall, and eyes forward." I felt a gun pressed up against my spine too. I immediately stood at attention because these muthafuckas certainly had my undivided attention now. Then the lights were dimmed over the crowd, and I could no longer see any of the men's faces. All I could see was their silhouettes.

What happened next amazed the fuck out of me. The man at the podium starting calling out numbers and shit, like we were at an art auction. He was saying, "Fifty thousand, sixty thousand, seventy thousand . . ." in a rapid tone.

I looked around strangely. Out of the corner of my eye, I noticed one of the girls who had been in the line, a beautiful redheaded white girl with perfect skin, standing out toward the front of the stage. She was turning around and around like she was showing herself off. The man kept calling numbers, and the men in the crowd were raising paddles and appeared to be bidding on her.

I could've fainted right then and there at what I finally concluded. *Oh shit! We are fucking being auctioned off to these men!* I screamed inside of my head. There were only about ten girls ahead of me. This was some sick shit, for real. That fucking Lamar had really sold me into a human trafficking ring. I couldn't believe that bullshit.

I watched as girl after girl was auctioned off to the highest bidder. Some bids went as high as two hundred thousand dollars. Who the fuck really paid that much money for the company of a woman? I knew from my days as a lawyer and from running in circles with some really wealthy men that these well-dressed businessmen were some of the freakiest and nastiest bastards when it came to sex.

They probably spared no expense because most of them were unhappily married with stiff-ass wives who didn't fuck them. These men used prostitutes and high-priced call girls to live out their wildest fantasies.

As I stood up there, I just knew deep down inside these muthafuckas were probably just like that. The mere fact that they were at a human auction told me a lot about their asses.

I was finally up on the chopping block, shocked and humiliated. The man at the microphone called out my entire profile—half-Korean, half-Black, finished law school, real hair, real tits, no kids. I almost threw up when I saw the muthafucka that had bid highest and won me for the night. Needless to say, I had to be forced off the stage to go with my new "one-night owner."

BEYOND MY
WILDEST DREAMS

I was forcefully given over to a fat, balding, ugly Chinese businessman who resembled the statues of Buddha I had seen around my home as a child. His cheeks made him look like a dead blowfish. It was unusual for Asians to be so overweight, and I immediately lost all respect for him. He looked horrible. I guess that was why he was there buying company, but even money couldn't help him.

"Yoshi. You beautiful woman," he said. "I see you Korean. Best lovers."

I had been told that his name was Mr. Chuan Wang. He asked me to call him Chuan. I wasn't planning on calling him shit. Instead, I was planning on trying to get the fuck away from him and making a run for it once again if I could.

Mr. Wang grabbed onto my arm tightly when the auctioneers turned me over to him. I had looked out into the crowd and saw the man who took me from Bryce and Lamar. He was the head muthafucka in charge, I guess.

Mr. Wang had to practically drag me out of the building because I was barely moving my feet on my own accord. When we got into that same parking lot I had come through when I'd first arrived, he stopped walking and we waited. He held onto my arm like he could sense that I wanted to run away. I guess he was used to this type of arrangement; most of the women he bought at auction probably showed resistance. I doubted very much that any of us was there voluntarily.

After we waited for a short period of time, Mr. Wang's driver finally pulled up in front of us in a black Bentley. Usually, I would have been overjoyed about being in such a beautiful luxury car, but it was much different for me. I mean, I used to own cars right up there with the Bentley I was about to get into with this fat, ugly, rich-ass man. But it didn't matter what car it was. I didn't want to ride in it at all. The driver got out of the Bentley and opened the door for Mr. Wang and me, but I couldn't move. I stood still. Even if I wanted to, I was unable to move from that spot.

"Something wrong, Yoshi?" Mr. Wang asked me.

"Yes. I don't want to go with you," I said, refusing to move. I thought I'd just try honesty and see where that shit got me.

"Ohh. Yoshi, you be careful. I pay. You come," Mr. Wang said, tugging on my arm roughly. He started smiling like I should be overjoyed by his presence. When he smiled that's when I saw how yellow and nasty his teeth were.

"I am here against my will," I blurted out, still trying to level with him.

"Not my problem, Yoshi. We go," he said in an irritated tone. Then he clicked his teeth, and all of a sudden two men were standing in front of me.

I knew they were there to help me get me in that car. I took one look at them and the weapons they held in their hands, and climbed into the back of the Bentley to face an uncertain fate.

Once inside the car, Mr. Wang wasted no time showing me that he wanted to get just what the he paid for. That bastard just wouldn't keep his fucking fat-ass frankfurter fingers off of me. He groped my tits and then my legs and ass. Then he stuck his hand up my dress and pulled my thong aside so he could fiddle with my pussy. That shit made me so uncomfortable.

After a few minutes I suddenly felt his fat fingers penetrate me. I instinctively snapped my thighs shut, crushing his hand. I always hated being groped. It made me feel dirty.

"You cooperate, or I report you to boss. He no be happy. You will be punished," Mr. Wang said when he felt my resistance.

I swallowed hard and reluctantly opened my legs. He rammed two and then three of his fingers inside of me. I was sickened by his nasty disregard for my body. But each time I thought I'd scream or slap the shit out of his nasty, fat ass, all I had to do was look at the driver and the passenger up front. I knew they were packing some serious heat, and that they wouldn't hesitate to spill my brains or guts all over the backseat of the car.

When Mr. Wang tried to put his tongue in my mouth, that was the last straw for me. He grabbed my face roughly and pulled it close to his. He opened his mouth to put it on top of mine, and the smell that came out of his mouth made me almost die. It smelled like shit mixed with fish.

I started squirming away from him, determined to keep him from putting his stink-ass mouth on mine. Now that was worth fighting for. There was no fucking way I was tongue-kissing that nasty-mouth muthafucka. I slapped his face away from mine so hard, I stung the inside of my own hand. I was sorry after I did it. He looked like he was caught off guard, and I was instantly shitting bricks for fear that he was going to have me killed.

"It was just reflex," I explained in a pleading voice. "I'm sorry. I don't kiss," I continued to explain in a real nice voice.

He busted out laughing like a big fat Chinese Santa Claus. I was confused as hell when he did that. He was definitely crazy. I looked at him strangely.

"I like that. I like to be rough," he said between his outbursts of laughter.

I was surprised that he said he enjoyed it when I slapped him. I just shook my head. He was obviously one sick-ass man.

He grabbed my hand and placed it down into his crotch. I closed my eyes and willed my brain to take me to another place mentally. He used my hand to rub his dick through his pants. I swear, he was rubbing for about ten minutes, and I could barely feel even the least little bit, if anything—not even a small bulge. *Oh my goodness.* I had never experienced no shit like that, and I had been around a lot of dicks in my time. No lie, his dick must've been the size of a Vienna sausage or like a newborn's dick.

He was grunting like a bear or some sort of animal as he forcefully groped himself using my hand. I was so disgusted and angry, I could feel a knot growing in the pit of my stomach. I was fuming inside. I swore right there in that car, if I ever ran into Bryce or Lamar ever again in life, I would purchase a gun and blow both of their brains out, even in public. I hated them both so much that whenever I thought about them and their all-out betrayal, my blood would rush with heat. It was the fire of my anger, and I was feeling it right then as this pervert had his way with my body.

Those fucking bastards, Bryce and Lamar, really could've left me in that van that day or just killed me, and I would've been better off than I was now. I wondered if Mr. Wang and all those people who auctioned off women for fun knew who I really was, and that two bounties loomed over my head.

I rubbed Mr. Wang for what seemed like another hour. I had his grimy handprints all over my skin, and all I wanted to do was take a long scalding hot shower.

As I rubbed his dick, I felt his cell phone in his pocket. That shit had become my motivation to keep rubbing his shriveled dick. I worked my hands over his dick and around his pants until I made his cell phone fall out of his pocket and onto the seat.

Mr. Wang had his eyes closed like he was enjoying it. He was so into my groping, he didn't even notice that his cell phone had fallen out of his pocket. I made a mental note to grab it before I exited that car, no matter what I had to do to get it. I knew that phone was my only hope of an escape.

"Yoshi, we have arrive," he said, like I couldn't see that the car had stopped. "We go. We have lots of fun."

I looked out the window to at least look for a street name, or if he had personalized gates or anything. I looked around, and I couldn't front, though. His estate was sick to death. Even in the dark I could tell that the grounds were well manicured and the house was huge. It had to be at least twenty or thirty thousand square feet, not including the land surrounding it. It was like some of my old clients' homes in Miami. Just seeing the house put me in a different state of mind.

Mr. Wang climbed out of the car first, and as soon as he did, I swiftly grabbed his cell phone off the seat. I held it up against the little clutch I had in my hand so I could hide it behind the bag's material. My heart was racing. I was so scared he would miss his phone and start looking for it and they would find out I had it. Still, it was a chance I had to take.

I was helped out of the car by one of Wang's little goons. I was holding on to that fucking phone for dear life. I just needed an opportunity to slip it inside the little clutch bag, instead of holding it outside of the bag. Once I had the phone secure, then I was going to need a minute alone to call Mario or somebody that could save me. At that point, I would've even called the police on myself, even though I was still a fugitive from the law.

After I got out of the car, I was handed over to Mr. Wang, who grabbed my arm like I was a piece of property and led me like an invalid who couldn't walk or see. We went into the house, and I was in awe. It was absolutely breathtaking inside, with all of the Asian-inspired artwork and decorations. I could tell from the looks of the home that Mr. Wang was not married and had no kids. That was probably why he was out here paying top dollar for pussy. I could also tell that he had servants for everything. I was about to become his sex servant. I was reminded of the days when I had money. I was kind of an evil bitch. Money makes muthafuckas turn evil.

Mr. Wang was feeling around in his pockets like he was trying to find something. I got nervous right away. I knew he was looking for his cell phone, so I tried to get his mind off it.

"We should hurry and get to bed," I purred, acting like I wanted him. I was hoping my deceit would work.

Mr. Wang smiled and stopped digging in his pockets. He wobbled his fat ass over to me, kissed me on the cheek, and asked me if I wanted a drink before we went to bed.

In my head I was screaming from him putting his nasty, cracked lips on my face, but I played it off. "Sure. What do you have?" I asked.

He showed me so many different bottles of high-priced liquors, I didn't know what to pick. I did know I definitely needed a fucking drink. I smiled and then I asked for a glass of Grey Goose and cranberry juice. When he gave it to me, I took that shit straight to the head like never before. I wanted to ask for the entire bottle and down that shit. I knew it was the only way I could survive having sex with a man like him. I had about four drinks before it was all said and done. As we headed up the huge, winding staircase, I felt like I was walking into impending doom.

Before I knew it, I was in Mr. Wang's bedroom standing in the middle of the floor stuck on stupid. The entire room was gold—even the walls and the floors. There were gold sheets, gold curtains, gold bedposts, and gold-painted furniture. You name it, and it was gold. It was the ugliest shit I had ever seen. I knew right away he had probably paid top dollar to have that fucking room decorated like that. He was not working with a full deck at all.

As I stood there with a case of the fucking creeps, he walked up behind me and whispered in my ear, his dragon breath killing my nostrils. "Take off everything," he said.

I lowered my head in shame. Then I slowly removed every piece of my borrowed, high-priced gear. I stood there on display for him, feeling like a feast about to be devoured by a hungry crowd.

Mr. Wang's sick ass bent down in front of me. He was huffing and puffing because he was so fat, and he started sniffing me like he was a dog. He inhaled deeply as he sniffed my hair, between my tits, my pussy, and my ass. It was just sick. I couldn't understand his need to smell me. I felt like shit was crawling all over my skin.

When he was finished taking in my scent, he slapped me on the ass real hard. That shit stung like hell, but I didn't even flinch. I was numb from all the shit I had been through, so I just stood there motionless and emotionless.

He walked over to the bed and tapped it, signaling me to come and get on the bed. I walked over to it robotically and sat down. He stroked my hair and pulled it out of the bun it was in. I could feel my long, thick locks spill over my shoulders like snakes. That's how I felt right then—like snakes were attacking me with each touch from his fingers.

"Lie down in middle," Mr. Wang demanded.

I just did as I was told and stretched my naked body out in the middle of his bed. I could smell the strong aroma of incense, but I didn't see any burning anywhere in the room. I had a blank stare on my face. I thought about the cell phone in my bag. Then I began trying to picture Mario's face or something pleasant, so I wouldn't start crying or screaming.

Once I was in the middle of the bed, Mr. Wang turned away from me and clapped his hands together three or four times like he was summoning a dog. I crinkled my face up to show my pure confusion. I didn't know if the clapping was a sign for me, or whether this crazy bastard was just displaying some sort of erratic behavior.

I quickly found out that he was doing the clapping to call in some of his goons. As if on cue, two men dressed from head to toe in all black rushed into the room to get to where I was lying. One of the slim Chinese men grabbed my left arm, and the other grabbed my right arm. They yanked me up toward the headboard.

I started flailing. "What are y'all doing?" I cried out.

They didn't answer. Instead, they stretched me out, and then they tied my arms to the bedposts.

"What the fuck! Get off of me!" I let out an ear-shattering scream.

I knew it was all for nothing, though. In that big-ass house that sat on that big-ass private estate, I knew not a damn soul on the outside would hear me.

They kept manhandling me, and I could hear chains jangling.

"What the fuck are you doing?" I asked frantically.

Then Mr. Wang's men put my ankles in some sort of leg irons. I had a fear of restraints after the whole transport van situation, so being tied up was making me absolutely crazy. Tears were running down the corners of my eyes. I kept looking all around, and then I noticed bondage and sadomasochistic paraphernalia on a little table next to the bed. This muthafucka was obviously into pain, bondage, and torture. No wonder this fat, twisted bastard had to pay for a piece of ass. I couldn't even imagine what he had in store for me.

My stomach started churning, and I started fighting against the restraints when I saw that stuff on the table. I was pulling my hands and trying to kick my feet, but my efforts were all for nothing. I was secured tightly to that bed. My mind was running a million miles a minute because I had no idea what to expect from that sick fuck now.

When the men all left, Mr. Wang started undressing himself. I watched, so I would know when he was coming for me. His body looked worse naked than it did with clothes on. He had a layer of hair on his chest and stomach that resembled a nasty carpet. The hair was shaggy and straight, covering him and making him look like a caveman or a monkey. His stomach protruded grossly and sagged over his pelvic area, and his dick, completely hidden by his stomach, was nowhere to be found.

Mr. Wang walked over to the bed, smiling and showing those yellow teeth. I started bucking again, but it was all for nothing once again. He was clearly amused by my efforts to get out of the restraints.

He laughed, and his gut jumped up and down as he did. Standing up over me, he bent down and put his face on top of mine.

"Ahhh!" I screamed and started squirming, but that was a big fucking mistake. As soon as I opened my mouth wide to scream, he stuck that nasty-ass tongue of his into my mouth. "Mmmm!" I moaned, fighting to move my head. It was such a disgusting experience. The rancid smell of his breath and his stinky saliva was making me want to vomit.

Mr. Wang held my head in place, so the harder I fought, the more pain shot through my neck. He shoved his nasty-ass tongue so deeply in my mouth, he was practically pushing it down my throat. I was gagging and felt like I would throw up.

When he finished, I could smell the stench of his saliva on my upper lip. I was racked with sobs by then, and my body was shaking all over.

Mr. Wang, breathing hard now, just ignored my body language and picked up a camera and took several pictures of me. Then he moved his head down to my tits and started sucking on them roughly. He was sucking so hard, I thought my nipples would start bleeding. I was in severe pain, which got worse when he decided to use his sharp, uneven teeth to bite my tender nipples. With the skin of my nipples between his top and bottom front teeth, he started grinding his teeth back and forth and making horrible animalistic noises as his sweat dripped on me.

I screamed so loud and bucked my body so hard, I felt dizzy.

Mr. Wang started laughing hard and reached down and stroked his puny little dick. He got up off the bed and got a long black cow whip off his torture table.

"Please! No, please . . . I will do anything!" I pleaded, pulling my arms and trying to lift my legs. I could feel the arm restraints cutting into my wrists as I continued to fight against them.

"Yoshi been a bad girl," he said. He picked up the whip and slapped me across my bare thighs with it.

"Arghhh!" I screamed out in sheer pain.

He hit me again, and this time I could feel welts rising on my skin.

"Pleasssse!" I begged, my legs shaking from the sharp pain. I was sobbing and begging him for mercy. I screamed and begged over and over again.

But I quickly realized that the more I screamed and pleaded, the more turned-on he got, so I stopped. I didn't want to give him the satisfaction, so I just bit down into my jaw and took the pain in silence.

When his sick ass realized that the whip wasn't getting a reaction out of me, he moved on to his next form of torture. I saw out of the corner of my eye when he picked up a huge, oblong object. I couldn't tell what it was, but he brought it over to the bed, put it between my legs, and forced it into my pussy so hard, I had no choice but to scream out. No human would've been able to take that kind of pain.

"Heeeellppp!" I hollered. I felt blood rushing into my face, and my heart pumped like crazy.

Mr. Wang continued to push the object into my flesh as hard as he could. It felt like whatever he was using to sexually abuse me would come through the top of my head. That's how far he was ramming it up in me. I was in excruciating pain. My abdomen felt like it would burst.

"Hellpp pleaseee!" I screamed some more as he grinded the object back and forth, which was stretching my vaginal walls to capacity.

Mr. Wang was smiling and grunting as sweat dripped from his body onto mine. He was clearly highly turned on by all of this sick shit. But, again, I stopped the screaming because the screams were fueling his satisfaction. As he did everything he could to bring me pain, I bit down on my bottom lip, until blood squirted from it.

When he finally took the object out of me, I felt relieved, but I knew he wasn't finished with me yet. By then, my thighs were shaking uncontrollably. I just knew I'd go into shock at any minute.

Mr. Wang definitely wasn't finished with me yet, and he was going to let me know it. He came and straddled his fat ass over me. I could barely breathe as his weight threatened to crush my chest. He lifted this fat stomach up and pulled on his nasty dick, trying to get it to grow at least an inch. Trust me, there was no helping that little shit.

After he got it semi-hard, he leaned forward and forced his dick up to my mouth. I kept my lips closed tightly, refusing him entry. Until he slapped the shit out of me so hard, I had no choice but to open my mouth. He then forced his dick into my mouth roughly, and the salty taste of his sweaty foreskin invaded my tongue, and the smell of his musty body entered my nostrils. With the combination, I started gagging, and that seemed to turn him on.

He leaned up and started pumping his dick in and out of my mouth like my mouth was a pussy. It wasn't that his dick was big, but the pressure from his weight slamming into my head gave me a severe headache. He repeated his pumping motion over and over again until he came all in my mouth.

That's when I couldn't hold it in any longer, and I started lurching my body up. Just as I did that, vomit spewed up out of my mouth like an erupting volcano. It was more than disgusting; it was revolting.

But Mr. Wang was loving it. He actually moved back and rubbed his dick all over the vomit and come mixture that was on my face and running down my cheeks. It was so sickening as he did that nasty shit, I think a piece of me died that night.

He got up and slapped me in my face. "You bad girl, Yoshi," he said, and then he slapped me again. My head was like a ping-pong ball, with him slapping me side to side over and over again.

Then he picked up a wet, rolled-up towel and began beating me on my body with it. I knew that Asians believed that beatings with wet cloth did not leave bruises. He beat me for the next twenty to thirty minutes. It was turning him on. He was like the devil standing right in front of me. Blood was on my nose and lips, and my legs and arms were burning with pain. I was so weak, I couldn't even control my head. And my breathing was labored too. I felt like dying.

Mr. Wang did his little clap thing again, and the men returned. They even screwed up their faces when they saw the condition I was in. They untied my legs, but I was too weak to kick or fight anybody. One grabbed the left, and the other grabbed the right, and they held my legs back, kind of like the stirrups at a gynecologist's office. They did this so sick-ass Mr. Wang could climb between them and lick my pussy. It was humiliating and demeaning.

He started licking me with his rough tongue. Then he started biting on my clit and my pussy lips. I couldn't even scream anymore. I just lay there being defiled.

Then I felt him stop. I thanked God, but it was too soon. He got on his knees and put his little dick inside of me and started grinding on me. I felt his fat stomach on top my stomach, and with every thrust, his skin slapped against mine in a disgusting way. His sweat covered my body, and I felt like snakes and worms were biting my skin. It was the most humiliating thing I had ever been through in my entire life.

When Mr. Wang was finished with me, he left me there. My wrists and hands were numb from being tied, and my body burned all over.

As hard as I fought it, I could not keep sleep from overcoming me. Within a matter of minutes and before I knew it, I was knocked out.

||||

I don't know how long I slept before I felt one of Mr. Wang's men slapping my cheek softly to wake me up. When I opened my eyes, there were three of them in the room, two of them by the bed to take care of me, and one cleaning up everything around the room. I could tell I looked a mess, from the way they were looking at me.

I moaned, which was all I had the strength to do. They untied my hands, and I immediately started flexing my wrists because they hurt so badly. One of them helped me sit up, and I swear I felt like I was a newborn baby, the way my back was just so slack and weak.

My mind was muddled. I was too fucked-up to even think about getting that cell phone out of the pocketbook. If I didn't know any better, I would have thought I was given some sort of drug before I went to sleep, but I couldn't remember.

They started washing me up with some sort of sweet-smelling soap. The men even brushed my hair back into a neat ponytail and put ointment on the little nicks and scratches I had sustained from Mr. Wang. I started feeling slightly better, but still like shit.

"What happens to me now?" I asked. My throat was so dry, the words came out gravelly.

"You go back," one of the men answered. He was working on me like a doctor, for real.

"Back where?" I asked. Shit, I didn't know if they were taking me back to the auction place, the house, or to that first apartment in Brooklyn.

"Back where you came from. Wang done with you," the man told me.

Well, that fucking much I could've figured out. I knew his nasty, fat ass was done with me because there was nothing else he could do to me. I mean, he had beaten and tortured me in every way possible. And to tell me they were taking me the fuck back where I came from was fucking ridiculous, since these bastards had no idea where I came from.

I knew one thing for sure—I had to get the fuck away from these crazy Asian people. I started thinking, *The next time I'm auctioned off, it could be to some high-paying crazy with a fetish to strangle or kill women. Who would know if I got killed and dumped some place?* I really still couldn't believe this whole human trafficking ring. And I also wondered just how lucrative it was.

I was helped up after they bathed me and made sure I didn't smell like sweat, come, or vomit. They retrieved my dress and shoes from where Mr. Wang had hidden them, and these men literally dressed me, like I was a baby.

I was weak from the hunger pangs tearing through my gut, and from being beaten and basically raped for hours. Mr. Wang's men gave me some water when I asked for it, but that was about it. That water hurt going down, and it landed in my stomach like a ton of bricks. That's how fucked-up I was—even water was a problem.

When I finished gulping down the water, I could tell it was time to go. One of them picked me up and carried me like a new husband would carry his bride. He carried me through the house and outside to a different car than the one I had come in. This time, a Mercedes-Benz CLS 550 would be my transport vehicle.

I had become so used to being in that dark-ass gold room that my eyes hurt in the daylight. I buried my face in the guy's chest and imagined it was Mario carrying me over the threshold of our future honeymoon suite. Tears started coming out of my eyes. I was just thinking, *Yoshi, you are better than this. You have to get out of this shit.*

The man dumped me into the back of the car, and then he climbed into the backseat with me. I didn't want to lay down, so I sat up. I wanted to see where they were taking me to try to commit some landmarks to memory. I planned to get the fuck out of this shit.

The other two men got in the front seats of the car. I could only pray that they would just return me in one piece and not take me somewhere, shoot me in the head, and end all the bullshit.

As we pulled out of the Wang estate, headed back to where I'd come from, I felt like opening the window and spitting on the grounds. That place was literally hell on earth. If I ever got free, I vowed to come back and set the entire fucking thing on fire.

PLEASE WAKE ME UP!

I clutched the small purse in my hand like it was the most precious gem on earth. Inside was the cell phone I had stolen from Mr. Wang, and I was just waiting for a right opportunity to use it. I knew I couldn't dare use it in the car. They all knew what type of ring I had been sold into. They also all knew that me and all the other women forced into the ring were looking for any and every opportunity to get away.

When we pulled up to the house where I had been prepared for the last auction, my stomach immediately knotted up. I knew that the process would probably be started all over again. The car stopped, and my heart felt like it had too.

The guy in the back of the car with me got out and opened the door for me. Those bastards had the child locks on, so I couldn't have gotten out if I wanted to. When he opened the door to let me out, something inside of me just fucking snapped. It was like a survival instinct again. I kicked that muthafucka in his face so hard. Then I kicked off those fucking shoes and took off running for the gates around the house.

The two men in the front seat didn't have time to react fast enough. I could hear them screaming as I let the wind pick up behind me. It felt like I was running fast, but my body was so weak and tired that I was really barely getting anywhere. They were screeching and screaming in their language and signaling to the other men placed around the house.

"Help! Help! Me!" I screamed as I continued to try to run. My chest, lungs, legs, arms and every inch of my body was on fire. I could hear feet beating the ground all around me. My dress was hitched up over my hips, and I could feel the ground scratching up the bottom of my feet.

Then I dropped my clutch purse. That's when I fucked up.

I stopped to pick it up, and before I could even stand back up, about twenty men surrounded me. I just stayed on the ground on my knees. I was sobbing like somebody had just died. As a matter of fact, that's how I felt on the inside. I knew I had to give up. I mean, what other choice did I have?

Several seconds later, one of the men from the house grabbed me by my hair.

"Ahhh!" I screamed out. I refused to grab onto his hands because I refused to let go of my purse with the cell phone in it.

"You fuckin' crazy?" the Asian goon said to me.

"Ahhh!" I hollered again as he tightened his grip on my hair. That shit hurt like hell.

"Get her calm down," another man said with his fucked-up broken English.

"Help!" I squeaked out weakly. Then I felt a sharp pain in my thigh. "What the fuck are y'all doing!" I screamed out.

All of a sudden I couldn't feel my legs, my arms and the pain in my head quickly subsided. "Help!" I whispered. I could barely feel my lips.

Shit started getting real blurry, and everything was spinning. I figured out then that they had stuck me with a needle full of some kind of mind-altering drug. I couldn't feel shit, and I was trying to use my mind to fight against the effects of the drugs, but it was a losing battle. I was being moved, but I couldn't scream or say anything. I could hear the faint sound of women speaking, so wherever I was, I knew I was around women. I had no idea what would happen next, but I couldn't even fight any longer. I finally just conked the fuck out. It was lights out, Yoshi, and there wasn't a damn thing I could do about it.

III

I had no idea how much time had passed when I woke up to water being splashed on my face. I started waving my hands in front of my face because I felt like I was about to drown. "What the…" I started and I inhaled deeply.

I finally focused my eyesight and noticed the two little Asian women who had taken care of me before standing next to the bed where I was laying. "What are y'all doing? What's going on?" I asked, trying to sit up.

I was gently forced back down. "Don't try to sit up. You not ready," the main handler said.

The other woman just looked at me pitifully, like she felt so damn sorry for me. I made a mental note of that too. Shit, I was still a lawyer. I was thinking, maybe she felt sympathetic and I could play on that if we were ever alone, and I would be able to get her to help me get away.

"What's going on?" I whispered. I was trying to look around to see where that clutch was. I knew they probably recycled those expensive-ass clothes, so I was praying they hadn't given my bag to another one of the girls to wear.

"You relax. We take care of you," the head woman said.

"I want to sit up. I want to get up off the bed. I don't need anybody to help me get washed up," I said in an irritated tone. I was sick of all these muthafuckas bathing me, handling me, carrying me, and fucking babysitting me. This shit was getting out of hand.

"No! You obey, or else you get reported," the head woman said in a nasty-ass voice.

The other woman was still just staring at me like she felt so sorry.

"Now you let us help. You take a bath and get ready. Only a few hours," the head woman said.

I looked around and saw about six men posted up around the room. I guess they weren't taking any chances on me trying to escape again. This was some serious shit.

The women helped me up, and just as I sat up, I heard a piercing scream coming from somewhere inside the house. My eyes stretched wide. "What the fuck was that?" I asked, startled.

"You mind your business. You get ready," the head woman said.

Now she was being nasty and getting on my nerves.

Then I heard the screams again. It sounded like some girl was being tortured or beaten. I mean, the scream wasn't just like a regular old scream. It was like someone dying or in agonizing pain.

I finally got off the bed and started walking, with assistance, to the same bathroom I had been in before. Once again, there was a bathtub full of flower water and candles lit all around. I couldn't even get relaxed in there if I wanted to. I was too fucking busy trying to come up with escape schemes to relax.

When I was undressed, the second woman looked at my body.

"He hurt you. Bad man," she said. She was talking about the residual marks and bruises left from that fucking animal, Wang.

I just nodded my head in the affirmative. Then I got into the bath. "*Ssst!*" I winced. The water felt good on my aching muscles, but my scraped-up knees and the little scratches on my skin was burning from all of the stuff in the water.

Finally, after I sat back and decided to try to get my mind right, the woman walked over and washed my back. She wet my hair and shampooed it. She was being so gentle and so nice; not like that bitch who was always with her.

"I can't stand to look at myself in the mirror," I said as she massaged my scalp. "I don't know who I am anymore."

She remained silent, only focusing on her job of making me pretty.

"Cut my hair."

It was an impulsive decision on my part, but I didn't want to ever look in the mirror and see me. I wanted the woman who was sold as a sex slave to look different.

"You want to cut beautiful, long hair?"

"Yes, please. Just do it. I can't bear to see myself anymore."

She hesitated until I looked up and pleaded with my eyes. "OK, I do it."

She had me turn and lean on the side of the tub while she cut my hair. As it fell, so did any reservations or doubts. I *knew* I was going to escape.

"You are so nice. What are you doing here?" I asked her, getting my game ready.

"I come from China. I have no family. I have to work here," the woman said.

"Did they sell you before too?" I asked, swallowing a big lump in my throat.

"Yes. I can't make money again. They make me work like this. I have to send money to my family in China," the woman said.

I guess after they had used her up, they decided to make her wash other women's pussies in order to pay off a never-ending debt. I knew how it was for some Asian women. They were sold into slavery like this for the sake of their families. That shit just infuriated me even more.

"I need help. I need to get out of here," I said. I grabbed her hands from washing my hair. I looked her in the eyes for a long while.

She refused to have eye contact with me, shaking her head from left to right.

I could tell she wanted to help me. "Please! I'm begging you. All I need is a phone. I won't let them know that you helped me," I told her. I started crying. I knew after this bath, I was going to be dressed up and auctioned off again, this time to God knows who.

"I cannot help. You will die if you try get away," she said.

She rinsed the soap from my new hairdo and moved away from me to get one of the plush towels. I was sobbing uncontrollably. I needed her help.

"Don't try to leave," she said somberly. She wrapped a towel around my body and one on my hair. She helped me get out of the bathtub, and we walked back out into the bedroom in silence. She gave me the same lotion, the same facial moisturizer, and the same type of underwear, just in a different color. I mean, this shit was all robotic and methodical. Then she laid out another stunning dress. This time it was a midnight-blue Dolce & Gabbana dress, and a different bag and shoes.

"Um, can I carry the same bag?" I said frantically. "Where is the bag I had?" I asked in a panic.

"There," she said, pointing over at a table.

The only thing was, the fucking table was located between two of the goons in the room to guard me. There was no way I'd be able to bust the cell phone out and put it in a different bag. I had to think of a way to get that fucking bag and cell phone.

"You sit," the woman told me. She was going to do my makeup and my hair.

I sat down and continuously eyed that bag. "I just need help," I whispered. I was still trying to appeal to her sensitivity to my situation, since she had been in my shoes.

"You have to obey. If you run, you will die. If you don't go to auction, you will die. If you embarrass the boss, you will die."

I crinkled my face in confusion. As she continued to style my hair, I could see through the mirror that she had tears in her eyes. "What do you mean?" I said softly.

"One girl was my friend. She was taken off the street and brought into the circle. She wanted to get away, and she tried over and over again. She kept getting caught and brought back. Then one night at one of the auctions, she started screaming out that she was there against her will. She started acting crazy, and when they tried to turn her over to a buyer, she spat in his face and slapped him. She was a huge embarrassment to the boss, and he had to apologize. The whole auction was messed up because most of the rich men there didn't want to take the chance of having a girl with all the problems. That night the boss did not make any money. We were all left with a free night. So that meant he had to feed us, and he lost thousands of dollars. My friend had to pay for her actions. We were all lined up outside. The boss came, and he screamed and screamed at us. Then my friend . . . she . . . " Her voice trailed off.

I was in shock that all of this time she had been just acting like she didn't speak good English. I was so confused by how clear she was telling me the story. "What happened to your friend?" I asked, wanting her to finish.

"She was pulled out of the line. The boss made her strip off all of her clothes. He humiliated her. And then right there in front of all of us, he pulled out his gun, made her open her mouth, and he put his gun in her mouth and pulled the trigger. Her brains splattered all over my face and my beautiful dress. He killed her not because he lost money, but because she had embarrassed him in front of all of those high-profile men. He has no regard for life and even less regard for women."

She was whispering close to my ear, since she was doing my hair. She was also crying. I was even crying. I felt so bad. That shit made me so fucking scared.

"They threw her in a dumpster. I saw her on the news, and I knew that her family would be devastated. She had people in China, including a little boy."

I was dealing with some cold-ass bastards.

"What am I supposed to do? I can't stay here forever. I can't end up like you, working for them forever, even after I can't sell any more pussy," I sobbed.

I felt like maybe I could trust her. "I have a cell phone in that bag," I whispered to her. "All I need to do is get the bag out of this room."

She stretched her eyes wide. "No! You get dressed," she said loudly. "You go to auction." This bitch was back to speaking like she couldn't speak good English.

I immediately regretted telling her the phone was in there. I put my head down and let the tears flow. I thought I could trust her. Now she was going to get a hold of that phone and I would be fucked.

I was dressed up again. The dress fit me like a rubber glove, hugging every curve, and the makeup was flawless, just like the last time. My new short haircut made me look like a fashionable vixen. I had been transformed into an Asian Halle Berry as I looked in the mirror. I didn't care if I looked beautiful or not, though. It was the same process as before.

That stupid bitch, the head handler, came back, and she and the soft-spoken woman accompanied me to the auction again. They had given me a new bag. The other bag with the cell phone in it was long gone. I felt helpless and hopeless.

The auction went the same way as the first time. Me and about twenty-five other beautiful women were forcefully herded into a line and put on display like pieces of property and examined to see if we were up to par. Then the bidding began.

This time two men, one black and one Asian, got into a serious bidding war over me. I was shocked to see that the black man was the winner. He wasn't that bad-looking either. When I was led down off the stage to meet him, I noticed a huge diamond pinky ring on his right hand. For some reason, the ring looked familiar to me. I had been around lots of rich men in my life, so that wasn't that strange.

I put a halfhearted smile on my face as he reached out his hand to take mine. I was surprised because I expected him to grab onto me like Mr. Wang did.

"Hello, Yoshi. I'm Gene," he said.

His voice was smooth, but I could hear a hint an accent at the end of his words. I didn't speak. I just nodded my head. I didn't know what the fuck to expect, and I wasn't trying to fake like I was happy to be there.

We climbed into the back of a Mercedes-Benz Maybach. When I sat down, I noticed he kind of kept his distance. That confused me, because I expected him to immediately start groping me like Mr. Wang did. Obviously this man had more class, which gave me a little bit of relief. I placed my clutch on my lap, and something inside scraped past my knee. I noticed he was looking out of the window, so I quickly took a peek inside the bag. My eyes widened, and my heart started racing. My breathing became a bit shallow. Inside the purse was the cell phone. That woman had helped me after all.

But now I was with another man, and in for who-knew-what. Once again, I would have to wait for the perfect opportunity to try to use the phone. I inhaled deeply and tried to will myself to stay calm. I would need to be completely on top of my game to find a spot to use this phone.

"We're here," Gene said. Then he said something to his driver in his native tongue.

This muthafucka was speaking French. For real, he sounded just like Sheldon Chisholm. It sent a strange feeling down my spine. I tried to smile, but my cheeks wouldn't cooperate.

"What's this place?" I asked, finally able to move my lips.

"It's a helipad. We are going to take a ride on my helicopter to a beautiful place," Gene informed me.

I was looking at him like he had four heads. "You mean we're going someplace else to have sex?" I asked. I knew why those men came to those auctions, and it damn sure wasn't to pay top dollar for a bitch to take a helicopter ride with them.

"Who says we have to have sex? I paid for your company. That is what your boss advertised," he said.

"So you don't want to have sex with me?" I asked for clarification.

"Why don't we get into the helicopter and go? That way you will be able to see what I have planned for you, Yoshi."

I didn't like the way he said that. I took comfort in the fact that I had that cell phone in my bag. I promised myself that once we got wherever we were going I was going to call Mario once and for all.

We climbed into the back of the helicopter. Once we were strapped in, I started feeling funny. I don't know if it was a womanly instinct, but I knew something wasn't right. The loud noise from the propellers made me jump.

Gene looked over at me and flashed a phony-ass smile. I was thinking, he was probably sicker than fucking Mr. Wang.

The helicopter lifted off the ground and got up in the air. I had turned my head and was looking out of the glass as the ground got smaller and smaller. I closed my eyes. I felt like praying but couldn't.

"Are you afraid of heights?" Gene screamed out, so I could hear him over the loud noise of the propellers.

I turned to face him to see what he wanted. When I turned around to give him eye contact and respond to his question, he gave me this cold expression.

"No, I'm not afraid of heights."

"If you're not afraid of heights, then why did you close your eyes?"

"No reason." I lied.

Instead of a rebuttal, he gave me this really weird facial expression. At first glance, he reminded me of a psychotic rapist or a fucking pedophile. I got the chills instantly. For a minute there I thought he was about to push my ass out of the helicopter. Thank God he didn't. A coroner would've been scraping me up off the ground for sure.

I turned my head to look out the window of the helicopter and tried to think of a way to escape, but, of course, my train of thought was interrupted. When I felt the helicopter descend to the ground, my heart started beating uncontrollably. I looked down to the ground and noticed that we were minutes away from landing on top of a building, which meant that we had reached our destination and I would be escorted off the helicopter the moment we touched down. I did not like that one bit.

My first thought was to resist and give these goons a hard time, but then I decided against it. It would've been just my luck that they'd knock me out and I wouldn't wake back up. I couldn't chance that, so I cooperated.

I was escorted off the helicopter, down one flight of stairs, and ushered into a penthouse-style apartment in less than three minutes. When I first stepped inside what appeared to be at least three thousand square feet of real estate, I was taken aback when I saw all the people in the living room area half-naked. Everyone in the place looked to be high on some substance or intoxicated from alcohol. Women were groping other women, and the men were fondling each other as well. It was a sight to see. If this wasn't Sodom and Gomorrah, then my name wasn't Yoshi Lomax. I just stood there in awe.

When Gene felt like I had seen enough, he quickly ushered me into one of the private suites within the penthouse. Inside the room was a king-size canopy bed. The satin comforter and bedsheets had to be every bit of one thousand thread-count. It was beautiful, but I didn't want to lie down on them. I wanted to get the hell out of there. All the shit I'd seen in the other room had given me some bad vibes.

"Stand over by the bed and get undressed. I'll be right back,"

Gene told me. And right after he walked out of the bedroom, his two bodyguards followed him out.

The moment they shut the door, my heart started racing. I knew I only had a few seconds to pull out the cellular phone and make the call to Mario. I rushed into the bathroom and locked the door. I stood behind the door with my back pressed against it. My heart was pounding so hard, it was making my ears ring. I knew my weight against the door wouldn't hold those thugs from busting down the door, but I did it anyway.

Scared to death of being caught, I opened up my purse and grabbed a hold of the phone inside of it. My hands were shaking like crazy, but I managed to dial all ten digits of Mario's cell phone number. To my surprise, his voice mail came on after the first ring. I damn near panicked.

"Shit! Shit! Shit!" I muffled underneath my breath. I almost went into a silent cry, but I convinced myself to hold it together, and said a quick prayer while I pressed down on the SEND button to call the number again.

My heartbeat grew more intense rapidly. I prepared myself to hear Mario's voice mail message again but prayed that I didn't. Ironically, this time his voice mail didn't come on at all. I didn't even hear the line ring, so I pulled the phone away from my ear to see if the call had connected, and when I saw that it had and the time was running, I put the phone back to my ear and held my breath. I didn't want any noise to prevent me from hearing anything on the other line. But unfortunately that didn't work. The phone line seemed like it was dead, so again I pulled the phone away from my ear to see if the line was still connected, and it was. So I knew someone had to be on the other end, and I was going to make sure of it.

"Hello, is someone there?" I asked, my voice trembling in barely a whisper.

"Who is this?" I heard Mario ask.

I could just picture his beautiful face all twisted up with a confused look but still sexy as hell.

My heart skipped several beats and when I heard his voice I almost lost my composure. I wanted to dive through the receiver of the phone that instant. I wanted him to save me from these fucking goons that had me captive.

"Baby, it's me, Yoshi!" I answered in whisper, tears immediately welling up in my eyes. It was like a real dream come true at that moment.

There was a little bit of a pause, like Mario couldn't believe his ears at first. Then his voice filtered through the line again.

"Oh shit! Yoshi, is this you for real?" Mario asked, excited.

"Yes, Mario, it's me, but listen," I whispered, looking around nervously, "I can't talk long."

"Why not? What's going on?"

I tried to hold back the tears, but I couldn't. That shit was falling like a rainstorm now. "Mario, I was kidnapped and brought to this place."

"Who kidnapped you? What place?"

"Two guys that hijacked the U.S. Marshal van to help the other prisoner escape while we were in Virginia. They were the ones who killed the marshals too." I continued to sob. I knew I must've sounded confused and all over the place. Mario didn't know what the hell I was talking about as I rambled through tears.

"Where are you?"

"I don't know." My sobbing sounded like whimpering.

"Whatcha mean, you don't know?" he sounded frustrated.

"All I know is that I'm in New York. That fuckin' animal, Lamar Patterson, brought me to New York and sold me to some Asian man, who is selling me for fuckin' sex," I whispered harshly, trying to get my point across. Then I paused before adding, "Mario, I need you to find me before they kill me."

"Baby, please stop crying. You gotta be strong until I'm able to find you. "

"You gotta hurry up." I begged. I was shaking all over.

"I'm on it, Yoshi, but you gotta help me out."

I heard him moving about. I assumed he was trying to find a pen and paper or something to record any clues I could give him about my whereabouts.

"Help you how?" I began to get impatient. It was like he didn't fucking understand what I was saying.

"You gotta tell me more about where you're at. Telling me you're in New York ain't helping me at all."

"Wait. I remember the guy from last night telling his driver to take me back to Long Island, so that's where the house has to be."

"Did he say where in Long Island? How long does the ride to the city take?"

Before I was able to respond to his question, I heard Gene and another man's voice outside of the bathroom door as they entered the bedroom suite.

"Where the fuck is she?" Gene asked in a frustrated manner.

I literally froze. "Oh my God! Mario, they're looking for me."

"Who is it?" Mario yelled through the phone. "Tell me a name, Yoshi!" Mario screamed into the phone.

"This guy's name Gene. Oh my God, Mario! I'm hiding in the

bathroom, and he's looking for me. I gotta go before he catches me on this phone. He will fuckin' kill me on the spot."

Mario yelled, "Wait—"

I had to hurry up and disconnect the call. With my hands shaking like crazy, I rushed over toward the toilet and flushed it, like I had just used it.

Meanwhile, Gene and his associate were pounding on the bathroom door.

"Yoshi! Yoshi! Open up now before I bust this gotdamn door down," Gene screamed like a maniac.

After struggling to turn the phone off, I wiped the tears from my eyes, and then I dropped the phone into a vase filled with a silk flower arrangement that sat at the right side of the large luxury Jacuzzi-type bathtub. To throw Gene and his goon off, I pretended to wash my hands and yelled back through the door, "Be out in a second." I couldn't even take a damn piss in peace, as far as these bastards were concerned.

Gene wasn't buying into my story, so his henchman kicked the bathroom door in without saying a word. The door busted open with a big bang, and the doorknob hit the bathroom wall abruptly, scaring the shit out of me.

I stood there frightened and didn't know what to do. It was clear that I was with another fucking crazy maniac just like Mr. Wang.

"Who the fuck were you talking to?" Gene didn't hesitate to ask me. He grabbed my face roughly, so he could look into my eyes. He was squeezing my cheeks so hard, the pain was crazy. I just knew he had already left bruises on my flawless face.

"I wasn't talking to anyone. I was praying," I lied, struggling to speak under his grip.

"That's bullshit, Gene," the goon with him yelled out, blowing up my spot. "She's lying. Look at her eyes. They're red, like she's been crying."

I rolled my eyes at him to let him know I didn't appreciate his instigating.

Gene squinted his eyes and let go of my face with a push. He pushed me so hard, I stumbled backwards and almost busted my ass on that marble floor. I thought when Gene let me go that he was finally satisfied with my story, but I was wrong. Gene wasn't finished yet. He asked me again who I was talking to, frantically scanning the bathroom, as if he expected a masked murderer to jump out of nowhere.

"I told—"

Before I could fully answer, he slapped the shit out of me, and a trickle of blood shot from my bottom lip because my lip hit up against my teeth.

"No, I'm not lying! I swear!" I cried out, holding my cheek. "I was praying out loud while I was sitting on the toilet." I was very tired of these so-called auction customers slapping me and abusing me.

Gene scanned the entire bathroom with his eyes again. I figured he was looking to see if anything was out of order, for a clue as to what I was really doing, since he didn't believe I was praying. Then he started tearing shit up in the bathroom. He opened the cabinets on the cherry wood sink and rummaged through them. Then he opened the medicine cabinets and started pushing shit out of it into the sink, and then he tore down the beautiful decorative towels that hung around.

When he didn't find shit out of order or suspicious, he snatched my pocketbook and emptied it out. My heart was pounding uncontrollably, but I remained calm. I knew he wouldn't find shit. The one place his dumb ass never bothered to look was in that fucking vase. I was proud of myself for thinking of putting the phone in the vase. That was quick thinking on my part and dumb on Gene's part not to check there.

Gene got tired of trying to prove me to be a liar and turned his attention back to the reason I was there in the first place—sex.

"Why do you still have your clothes on? Didn't I tell you to be undressed when I got back?" he said to me with an attitude, clearly disgusted with me.

"I was getting ready to do that, but I had to use the bathroom really bad."

Gene slapped me again, and I let out a little whimper. I wanted to scream at him and say, "What the fuck was that for?" But I just held my cheek and gave him the look of death instead.

Then Gene grabbed me by the arm roughly, like he was about to take me out of the bathroom. He put his face close to mine instead and was talking all up in my face. "Don't do that again unless you ask me for fuckin' permission. I own you right now. Now you gonna do what I say."

Before he forced me back into the huge bedroom, I really did start praying silently that God would just help me get out of the situation I was in. I also prayed that Mario would come up with a miraculous way to find me. I prayed that I would get another chance to get back to that phone. I also prayed that all of these sick muthafuckas would just drop dead. I couldn't get Mario's voice out of my head. I could hear him over and over again telling me that he would find me. I really believed him too.

"Take off your fuckin' clothes right now, I said!" Gene growled.

But he didn't even give me a minute to move. He grabbed my dress and ripped it by the zipper. I heard the material tearing and pieces of it shredding. The entire dress just dropped off me and fell around my ankles. He had definitely changed from the refined businessman he acted like at the auction.

"Get on your fuckin' knees!" he yelled, grabbing me and forcing me down to the floor roughly.

Gene's abusive ways snapped me back to reality. I started doing as I was told. I had no other choice. I was on my knees, and my face was right in front of his crotch area. I watched him fumble with his zipper, and then I was staring straight at his huge black dick. I knew what that meant. Tears leaked out of the corners of my eyes.

Gene grabbed my short hair roughly.

I couldn't even say, "Ouch!" That's how much pain and distress I was in.

Then he yanked my head and forced my face into his dick. "Suck my dick, bitch," he said gruffly.

I reluctantly opened my mouth and accepted his thick, salty-tasting flesh. I almost gagged. As soon as his dick was in my mouth, Gene started moving rapidly, like he was fucking me in my mouth. Just like Wang, he was acting like my mouth was a pussy.

I felt like my neck would break, as hard as he was pumping into my face. Saliva was leaking out of my lips and dripping onto his dick, running down my chin. Most of the time when he thrust hard, I felt like I was gagging and like I would throw up. I was in pain, but Gene was in ecstasy. It was replay of the shit Mr. Wang had done to me.

Gene was grunting and pumping, and I thought about biting down on his dick and trying to bite that fucking thing off. But I knew he probably had about twenty of his little henchmen outside the door who would kill my ass if I did that. I pictured the pain he would be in if I did decided to bite down on his dick. Just the thought gave me a little satisfaction, but the thought of what would happen to me didn't sit right with me.

So I just stayed there with my knees burning on the hard floor, and my neck killing me, and let Gene fuck my mouth until he came.

He pulled his dick out and squirted his come all over my face. Then he held my head back so one of his goons could snap pictures of me with the come dripping over my lips, eyes, and nose. "Now that's the fuckin' money shot," he gasped, out of breath from coming.

They laughed. I was humiliated. This shit was over the top, and I was really getting to my wits' end with all of this abuse.

"Now, I got the real shit for your ass," Gene said to me.

I couldn't even imagine what more he wanted to do to me.

He was smiling like he already knew what he had in mind was probably sick and twisted. "Get up now. It's show time," he said as he grabbed me up off the floor.

THE PRICE OF PUSSY

Gene forcefully pushed me out of the bathroom and made me go over by the huge king-size bed that sat in the middle of the bedroom. I didn't even try to cover my stark naked body; there was no use now. I had already been humiliated and defiled. I knew I was about to be used and abused by God only knew who, and God only knew how. I could only imagine that it would be some sick, kinky shit.

As I stood there awaiting my fate, two naked Caucasian women walked into the bedroom and sprawled out across the bed. I looked around, confused as hell. I eyed them carefully and suspiciously. One of the women, a skinny blonde, wore a strap-on dildo that had to be at least twelve inches long, while the other woman, a curvier brunette, held a whip in her right hand. Both of them looked like extras from the Playboy Mansion, with their fake tits and ass implants. I could tell right off the bat that they were into that bondage type of sex, and I was about to be their play toy.

I closed my eyes to block out everyone around me, so I could think about the conversation I'd just had with Mario. Replaying his voice was the only thing that was going to get me through what was in store for me. The fact that I had just talked to Mario gave me a sense of hope that he was going to find a way to save me. I just wished I could have given him more information on my whereabouts. I was hoping, by telling him that I was somewhere in Long Island, he'd be able to track me down somehow.

"Get over there, Yoshi! I already told you, it's show time," Gene yelled out, pushing me forward until I fell onto the bed.

Those two white bitches didn't waste any time coming at me. They swooped down on me like animals. The brunette immediately took that whip and slapped me on my naked ass with it. I could tell they had done shit like this before.

"Ouch! Bitch!" I hollered. I really wanted to grab her by the hair and fuck her up.

She hit me again, this time harder.

"Don't fuckin' hit me with that shit again!" I screamed at her. I was dead serious. I wasn't going to let this bitch just hit on me. I was kind of powerless because I was laying on my stomach on the bed, a position that didn't give me much power to fight.

Gene laughed at my angry outburst. This sick muthafucka liked it.

She hit me again as the other girl leaned over me and held my arms down, and Gene stood by the bed and held my feet down. I started bucking like crazy. That fucking leather cow whip stung like a muthafucka on my delicate skin.

The bitch finally stopped hitting me. Then I felt somebody behind me spreading my ass cheeks apart.

"Please don't!" I screamed out. I wasn't into ass-fucking nobody that I didn't know. I started squirming like crazy, trying to get away.

Gene laughed again. It was like anytime he thought I was in pain or some shit it turned him on. I realized the more I screamed, the more turned-on and excited he got.

The next thing I felt was them putting some kind of lubricant up and down my ass-crack.

"Please!" I begged. That anal shit hurt like a hell if a person didn't take their time, and I knew these people were not interested in taking their time, or whether or not I was in pain. I was squirming and trying to get away, but it was useless against the three of them.

The blonde climbed up behind me. I saw her through the mirror across from the bed stroking that fucking strap-on dildo like it was a real dick. When she finally straddled me from the back, she put her weight down on my legs. At that point, Gene let go of my legs and came around in front of me.

I tried to kick my legs, but this blonde bitch was sitting back on my thighs and I couldn't move.

Gene got on the bed and pinned my arms down with his knees as he forced his dick back into my mouth. I was still on my stomach, so it was a helpless position. The blonde forced her strap-on into my asshole. I was being penetrated from the front and the back. I couldn't scream, and I felt like I was choking from his long, thick dick. I couldn't breathe either. I was sure I would die.

The pain radiating through my asshole was unbearable. That bitch was going crazy, pumping into my asshole like she had a real dick and could really feel the sensations. They had me like a ping-pong ball. She would pump me from the back, and Gene would pump me from the front.

My neck was in a bad position, and I felt pain all over my body. What they were doing to me was unnatural. They had my body contorted like a damn pretzel. I was crying, which made it worse as I tried to get some air.

Gene was grunting in pleasure. So was the blonde.

Finally, Gene came. "Urgggh!" he screamed out as the climax radiated through his body.

The brunette rushed over to him and started drinking his come and letting him put it all over her lips and tongue. I was just relieved to have his dick out of my mouth. The girl pulled the strap-on out of my ass right at the same time that Gene had pulled out of my mouth.

I felt immediate relief, but not for very long. Gene wasted no time making me turn on my back, so he could fuck me in the pussy. He came around and pushed his dick into my pussy roughly.

The blonde took off her strap-on and climbed over my face.

"Lick my pussy, bitch," she said, and she tried to lower her musty pussy over my mouth.

I moved my head left and right trying to resist having her vagina near my mouth, but when I did that Gene bent down and bit into my nipple so hard, I screamed out.

"Do as you are told, Yoshi, if you want to leave here alive," he grunted.

I reluctantly opened my mouth and stuck out my tongue, and the blonde bitch lowered her stankin' pussyhole right onto my mouth and started grinding on my face like I was a fucking nigga eating her pussy.

Sick bitch.

The abuse went on for what had to be hours. I ate so much pussy, got fucked in the ass and pussy until I really felt like I was almost dead.

Gene was the only man I had ever been around whose dick never went down. Even after he ejaculated over and over again, his shit never got limp. His dick was hard the entire night.

To make matters worse, after Gene and those bitches were done with me, about six of Gene's henchmen came in and fucked me. They all took turns. They turned me in every position imaginable. My pussy was dry and raw when they were finally done. All I could do was lie on the bed in a fetal position. My legs were shaking like crazy, and my abdomen throbbed.

I had never been through shit like that in my life. I was in so much pain, I couldn't even get myself together right away. Pain and all, I still kept thinking about how I was going to get back into that bathroom and get that phone. It was my only hope of making it away from all of these sick fucks alive.

After they were all done using and abusing me, Gene ordered some of his bastard henchmen to dress me and take me back to the boss. As they helped me lift my weak body up off the bed, I begged one of them to let me use the bathroom. They ignored me as they laid out a new dress for me to wear.

I continued to plead with them. "Please. My bladder is going to explode after all of that," I said, putting on my saddest face and using my baby voice.

The two men dressing me talked about it for a few seconds, and I guess they decided there was nowhere for me to run or hide even if they did let me go.

"You can go take a quick piss and even a shit if you have to. But hurry the fuck up—And don't try to pull any stunts," one of them said, showing me his silver pistol.

I dragged myself back into the bathroom as fast as I could. I closed the door and rushed to the vase. I dumped it out and retrieved the phone. I was being very careful not to make too much noise. I stuffed the phone into the side of my bra under my arm, so they wouldn't see it.

Then I forced my piss out as fast as I could. My asshole and pussy were on fire. I had to get the hell away from these people.

Within a few minutes of me being in the bathroom, they started banging on the door, just like I knew they would. That was why I hadn't even tried to take a chance and call Mario again. I knew I had to wait for another prime opportunity.

"I'm ready," I said, snatching the door open.

Both men eyed me suspiciously, but neither of them thought to search me. I could feel the phone digging into the side of my breast. That feeling gave me so much comfort because that little piece of technology was my only hope.

"Let's go," one of the men said.

He went to grab my arm on the side where the phone was, but I jumped. "Please hold this arm. Gene worked me over pretty bad, and this arm is very sore," I said in a pleading voice.

The other guy said, "You know Gene is a wild boy. He probably did fuck her arm up."

The first henchman agreed and changed arms.

I exhaled a sigh of relief. Now I was sure I would make it out of there with the phone. But I wasn't sure where I was headed next, or if I'd ever get a chance to call Mario again.

GOTTA GET AWAY

During the entire helicopter ride back to the Long Island house, I replayed Mario's voice in my head.

"Yoshi, where are you? Yoshi, I will find you," Mario had said to me, and I could hear the concern lacing his words as he kept asking me where I was.

I felt so fucked up that I couldn't even tell him where I was after all that time. All I could tell him was Long Island. That probably wasn't helpful in the least bit. I knew a little bit about New York, and knew that Long Island was a big fucking place with a bunch of little towns.

But one thing eased my thoughts. I was glad that I at least got to tell him that I hadn't killed those U.S. Marshals. It was important to me what Mario thought of me, since he was the only one there for me toward the end of my other ordeal. Mario was such a man. I kept hearing his words that he would find me "no matter how long it took." That kind of made me smile to myself, but I was careful not to let any of those bastards that worked for Gene see me smiling, before they started asking why. I hated them all, especially because I could still feel the inside of my pussy throbbing from all of their sexual abuse.

When the helicopter landed there was a black Benz waiting for us on the helipad. I was practically dragged out of the helicopter and forced into the backseat of the Benz.

We drove for about another thirty minutes. At first, I was thinking wishfully that they were going to take me somewhere and let me out of the car, so I could runaway. Don't ask me why I even dreamed that shit up, because it wasn't going to happen.

Sure enough, I looked out of the window of the car and started seeing familiar shit, so I started taking mental notes of the scenery. Then when we pulled up to the familiar house in Long Island my stomach knotted up. All I could imagine was being washed up by those two Asian bitches all over again, dressed up again, and sold off at another auction to another sick fucking rich bastard with deviant sexual fantasies. The thought of the whole thing made me feel like I had to take a shit or throw up.

I swallowed hard as the car stopped in front of the house. Gene's workers got out to open the door for me and to basically prepare themselves for me to wild out. I just got out of the car calmly. I didn't even have any fight in me to start kicking and screaming and trying to run again. I was so out of it and just focused on making another call to Mario, I just calmly got out and went with the boss's guards.

I was ushered inside and turned over to the two women who bathed me and dressed me up. I hated even the sight of those two bitches. But I did remember that one of them had helped me out before. Still, a sense of panic came over me thinking about the process they were about to put me through again.

I dragged my feet and followed them. I just knew they were about to prepare me for another auction, but instead of being led to the room I usually went in to get dressed, they led to me another set of rooms.

"You rest tonight. You body need rest," the head bitch said, with her barely-speaking-English ass.

I immediately got excited inside, but I was careful to hide my feelings. Nothing was ever as it seemed in the business these people were in.

She used a key to open a bedroom door, led me inside, and handed me some fresh, clean, comfortable-looking pajamas.

"Make sure you take rest. Sleep," the other lady said in her soft, girlish voice. She was the nice one who had given me the phone in the first place.

I winked at her and said I would get rest.

They left and locked the door behind them. This shit was serious enough that they were locking bitches in rooms just to even get rest. That told me that they knew everything they were doing was just wrong.

Once they were gone and I felt like I was alone, I looked around the room. There were four full-size beds in the large room, all made up, except for one. I squinted my eyes in the dimly lit room and noticed that there was a girl asleep in the bed across from the one I set my stuff down on. The chick was snoring. I immediately knew how she felt. She was probably exhausted from some sick sexual-abuse ordeal she had been through. I was happy she was sleeping, and that I was alone.

I took off my clothes and changed into the pajamas they'd given me. I put the cell phone under the pillow until I could see if there were any cameras in that room. I tore the room up looking for hidden cameras. I looked in all of the obvious places—up at the ceiling, in the lamps, and near the electrical outlets. Then I looked in places I had heard that spies and DEA agents hid cameras—like around mirrors, under tables and chairs, and near television cable boxes.

I searched and searched and didn't find anything. I was baffled, knowing the type of people I was dealing with. Strangely enough, there were no cameras anywhere in that room. Although that was almost unbelievable to me, I was happy as hell.

I let out a long sigh of relief. My hands were shaking with anxiety, but I finally felt safe enough to call Mario again. The one problem was the girl across the room. I had no idea whether or not she was put in there to spy on me, or whether she was really just another girl in there sleeping.

I walked over to her to take a peek. I wanted to see if her eyes were fluttering or if there was any sign that she was really awake and faking sleep. I examined her closely. From what I could tell, that bitch was knocked the fuck out. I felt comfortable that she was really asleep, but I kept my eyes on her the whole time from across the room as I retrieved the phone from under the pillow and dialed Mario's number again.

I was praying silently that he answered quickly because I didn't know how much time I would have to talk to him. "C'mon, Mario," I whispered. I bit my bottom lip. Sure enough, it was like he was waiting for my call because the phone barely rang three times before I heard his voice filtering through the receiver.

"Hello," he answered.

I was so glad to hear his voice. It made my insides warm with relief. "Mario?" I whispered. Just saying his name made me start to cry again. I wanted to be in his arms right then.

"Yoshi, I been waiting for you to call me back. Do you know

where you are now?" he was whispering, like he thought the people who had me captive might be able to somehow hear him too.

"No. They brought me back to the same big house that I keep coming to over and over again. The one I told you about that's in Long Island somewhere. They keep on bathing me and dressing me up." I was trying to stay calm enough to get my words out, but the sobs were overcoming me. "Mario, they are making me do things that I can't even talk about. I need you to find me. These people are sick bastards."

"Calm down. The phone you on doesn't show up on my caller ID. I don't know why. Where did you get the phone from? What is the number?"

"I don't have much time," I whispered. "There's an Asian guy named Wang and, um, a black guy named Gene. I've been driven in a couple cars, a Bentley and a Benz. Please, you gotta save me, Mario. They are abusing me, and they will try to kill me."

"I am going to save you, baby. I called the FBI, and they are aware of your last call. You gotta stay on with me, so they can see what cell tower that phone is hitting off of and find what area you're in."

"I am in Long Island, but I don't know where. Every day we go to a different place for the auction. I think it's in Manhattan, because when we go, I can see the Empire State Building in the distance."

"Yoshi, I'm going to put the FBI agent on the phone, okay?" he said.

I didn't know how to feel. Really, I didn't trust any cops or federal agents, but what choice did I have? The only reason I hadn't called the cops myself was because I didn't think they would believe me, number one. And, number two, I didn't think they would ever be able to find me, the way the boss had his shit set up.

"Okay," I said to Mario. At that point, I didn't give a fuck who he put on the phone if they could help me.

"Ms. Lomax, we are trying to locate you, but you have to help us too," the FBI agent said in a gruff voice. His voice didn't give me any comfort, and something about it made me feel eerie inside.

"Anything you need," I said.

"We need to know what happened in Virginia with Lamar Patterson," he said.

Even though I couldn't believe or understand why he would be asking me about Lamar at a time like this, I still told him everything. I was rushing to get the words out of my mouth about how Lamar got broken out of the prison van, how Bryce and the others had killed those marshals in cold blood, and how Lamar had traded me for a ticket out of the country.

I was speaking so fast, my mouth was dry as hell. I knew I didn't have much fucking time to be on that phone. There was no telling when the people in that house would come back to get me for the next auction.

"Okay. We believe you based on some of the crime scene evidence. We are trying to pick up on the cell signal, but it seems the phone you have is one of those disposable track phones and is not linked to a service provider."

The agent's words hit me like a punch in the gut. When he said that shit, my heart felt like it had dropped down into the pit of my stomach. I had started off the conversation with hope that I would be traced and found, but those hopes went out the window when he said that shit about the cell phone towers.

"Please let me speak to back to my boyfriend. If you can't save me, I at least want to speak to him as much"—I stopped talking when

I heard something outside of the door.

At first I thought it was just my imagination fucking with me, because I was so paranoid. But then I heard a noise again and this time I was sure it was coming from outside of the door. I pulled the phone from my ear for a minute to listen more closely. I had stopped talking to Mario and was silent while I listened. I still could hear him screaming my name out through the phone, but I didn't dare say anything as I kept listening real closely, trying to decipher what noise was coming from outside the door.

As the noises got louder and closer, I suddenly realized it was footsteps I was hearing, and those shits were slowly but surely getting closer to the room. I could also tell it was more than one pair of feet rumbling toward the door.

My eyes bugged out real big when I finally knew for sure what was going on. "Oh shit! Mario, I gotta go," I whispered nervously, placing the phone real close to my mouth.

"Wait, Yoshi! Don't hang up yet! I need some info—"

I had to think about my safety, so I cut the call short and forcefully stuck the phone between the mattress and box spring of the bed. I swallowed hard and tried to will myself to be calm. "Calm down, Yoshi, calm down," I said to myself. I could just feel the worried look on my face, and I tried to hurry up and erase it off my face.

I rushed under the bed covers and tried to slow my rapid breathing, so I could fake like I was sleeping.

Finally the footsteps stopped. I knew they were in front of the door. My heart felt like it would come up into my throat, and my stomach was in knots.

The next thing I heard was a loud crash that made me jump. The door was busted open with a crashing sound by a group of men.

Speaking in their native language, their voices sounded angry and frantic. I could tell that whatever they were saying wasn't good. I knew they were probably saying something about me, but I was sure hoping they were coming to get the girl across the room.

I squeezed my eyes shut really tight, hoping and praying they weren't coming in there for me. The girl across from me had already jumped up when the door was busted open. She looked dazed and confused and was probably just as scared as I was.

I pulled the cover over my head, wishing I could just fucking disappear. "God, please don't let them be here for me," I mouthed silently.

Suddenly their voices in that fucking annoying-ass Asian dialect seemed to be all around me on every side, and coming from every angle around the bed I was in. I didn't have to question it anymore; there was no more doubt about who they were there to get.

Then their presence surrounding me turned in to actual hands touching me roughly, bearing down on me and yanking on me. They were yelling something, but I couldn't understand them. I could tell they were angry, and that whatever was going on, it wasn't good.

THE SHOCK TREATMENT

As the henchmen continued to yell and confer about my fate, the blanket was snatched off me as I cowered under it. There were four huge Asian men over the bed barking orders at me in Cantonese. One finally grabbed me out of the bed roughly, and the others started to tear up the room like they were searching or something.

"Please! What is going on?" I screamed, trying to act dazed and confused.

I wanted them to think I had been asleep, but it wasn't working at all. Two of them grabbed me and started dragging me out of the room, and the other two started tossing shit around in the room, like they were searching.

As they dragged me toward the hallway, I screamed, "Please! Let me go! I didn't do anything! Get off of me! They told me I could rest tonight!"

When I got to the doorway of the bedroom, I stretched my arms and held onto the doorframe, digging my nails into the wood. One of the men pried my fingers off the door, and they kept dragging me.

"Get off of me!" I hollered, kicking and screaming like a maniac. "Let me go!" I belted out at the top of my lungs. Sweat covering my body, I was bucking like a wild animal and trying to bite them. I was kicking them and dropping my body weight down so they couldn't carry me.

All of my fighting efforts were to no avail. They just kept dragging me to wherever they were taking me.

When we arrived at a big red door, I hollered out, "I'm not going in there!" But I knew better; I didn't have a fucking choice. They were taking me behind that scary-ass door anyway, whether I liked it or not.

The door finally flew open as we stood outside of it, and I started going even crazier. I honestly felt like a mental patient, from the way I carried on. The two men dragged me into a dimly lit room, and I saw a huge desk in front of me.

"What is this? Get off of me!" I screamed some more.

To tell the truth, I was scared as hell of this whole scene. It wasn't like they were taking me to the ladies to be bathed for the auction. This was some other shit.

I looked in front of me at the huge, king-size desk. A man sat behind it, his back turned. I shut up for a minute as he turned around, and I saw it was the man from the night Lamar had sold me. It was the boss. He had a real serious look on his face, like he could kill me with his eyes. A cold sweat broke out on my hot body as the men maintained their death grip on my arms.

"Yoshi, Yoshi, Yoshi. They told me you wouldn't be a problem when they turned you over to me, but from the first day I met you, I knew you would be trouble. But with such a beautiful face and gorgeous body, I also knew you could make me a lot of money. I am shocked at what I just found out, Yoshi. Really, I am more disappointed," he said grimly.

I was looking at him with a real confused look on my face. "I-I don't know what you're talking about," I stammered.

"Don't speak!" he screamed, slamming his hands on his desk and scaring the shit out of me.

His face was turning red. I could tell this was some serious shit I was in right now. This muthafucka looked like he could just eat me for dinner right then and there.

"You are a liar! You stand in my face and lie!" he screamed, blood rushing to his face again, turning him a fuchsia-looking color.

He plopped back down in his big swivel chair and moved aside, so I could see a screen he had been watching behind his desk. I squinted my eyes to see.

"Bring her over, so she can get a better look at herself," he said, and the two men dragged me closer to his desk.

My mouth dropped when I looked at the screen. I mean, I felt like all of the blood drained out of my body. I watched myself undress in that room before picking up the cell phone and calling Mario. I started to cry as I heard my voice filtering through the room telling Mario everything. I was so sure there were no cameras in that fucking room. I should've known better. I kept my eyes on the screen.

"So your boyfriend Mario is trying to save you, huh?" the boss asked me.

I couldn't even answer him. I was aware that my body was shivering at that moment. "You just dragged poor Mario into this now. We will find him, and we will kill him. How do you feel about putting your boyfriend in danger, Yoshi?" he asked.

I was shaking my head back and forth and crying hysterically. "I'm sorry. I won't do it again," I managed to say through my dry lips.

"I know you won't! You will be taught a valuable lesson!" he growled, his voice ringing in my ears.

"Take care of her! You know what to do—the max!" he instructed.

"Please . . . what is that?" I asked frantically, whirling my head around.

All of the men's faces were stoic. When the boss said "the max," that shit sounded serious. I wondered if that was their code word for death.

"Get her out of my sight!" the boss hollered.

Once again I was being dragged, and once again I was putting up a fight. I wasn't going out without a fight. I kept kicking and screaming until we arrived in what appeared to be the basement of the house. It was cold and dark in the room they took me into.

"Help!" I screamed, but I knew nobody could hear me.

It was like once we got down there, those men turned into devils too. I guess they were tired of all my yelling, kicking, and screaming.

One of them slapped me so hard, blood shot out of the spot on my lip that Gene had busted previously.

"Close your fucking mouth," the Asian goon said in a horrible accent.

I just knew I was going to die, and I didn't care anymore. So I spat in his face, letting all my blood out on him.

He screwed up his face and wiped away my bloody spit and slapped me again. This time his slap was extra hard, and it knocked me over. The other man dragged me over to a wooden armchair, but I stiffened my body to keep them from putting me in it.

One of them punched me in the stomach so hard, my body folded. When I doubled over, they forced me down into the chair. They immediately strapped my hands with metal cuffs to the arms of the chair, and my ankles were shackled to its legs.

"Help!" I screamed again. I kept struggling, but it was to no avail.

I looked over and saw some wires attached to some kind of contraption that resembled a car battery and jumper cables. Just as my eyes got wide, I felt water being poured over my head. I started thrashing because I felt like I was going to drown. Plus, that water was cold as hell.

The men laughed at me. Then one went over to that contraption and came back to me. The other one ripped off my pajama top and exposed my bare breasts. He grabbed one of my nipples and smiled. The man with the contraption came over with the jumper cable-looking thing and clipped the metal clamps onto both of my breasts.

"Ahhhhhh!" I screamed out from the pain of the metal pinching my delicate skin.

As soon as I opened my mouth, a huge wad of fabric was stuffed into it, and a piece of duct tape was forcefully wrapped around it to hold it in place. Now I couldn't even scream from the pain that radiated through my breasts. Then the man walked back over to the box that looked like a battery and flipped a switch.

My eyes grew wide as I felt a burning surge of electricity rip through my body. "Mmmm!" I screamed under the mouth gag. Piss ran down my legs in response to the pain and shocks. I could feel the electric shocks making my body shake. I felt like my flesh was being cooked.

They stopped the electric shocks for a minute, and my body went kind of limp. My head hung down, and I couldn't even lift it.

"You ever disobey again?" one of the men asked. When I didn't answer, he turned the electricity on again.

"Mmmmm!" I hollered again. My body bolted upright and strained against the shocks. I could feel snot or blood running out of my nose this time. My nipples were frying. I could've sworn I could smell my flesh really cooking.

The men were smiling at their handiwork and finding amusement in my pain.

They finally took the gag out of my mouth and started asking me questions about Mario. Every time I refused to answer them, they turned up the electricity and shocked me until I was half dead. I refused to tell them anything about Mario because I knew they would try to kill him. After a while I couldn't even hold my head up, so I started lying. I started giving them fake addresses and fake last names.

When they thought they had all of the information they needed on Mario to find him, they stopped the shock torture. They unshackled me, and my body slumped out of the chair onto the cold, wet floor. One of the men lifted me up over his shoulders and carried me down a long, dark, moldy-smelling hallway. There was no way I could fight anymore. I didn't even bother to try.

After a while of walking, the man stopped. My eyes were barely open, and all I could see, from the way he was carrying me, was the gray floor. I heard keys tinkling, and then I heard a loud clanging noise as a door opened.

I was then dumped onto a thin, bare mattress in a small, dark, damp room that resembled a prison cell. I moved my head around to take in the environment they had put me in. There was nothing in the room except that horrible, dirty mattress I was on and a single metal toilet in the corner. The light dangling from the ceiling was dim and raggedy and looked like it would fall down on my head at any minute.

When I was serving my time in Virginia, I was in a prison cell in better condition than the room these Asian bastards had put me in.

"Please, I'm thirsty," I pleaded.

"You get nothing. You stay here few days until you learn lesson," one of the men said.

"Please. I'm sorry. I won't do it again. Please, just have mercy on me," I begged in a weak voice.

They just stared down at me like I was a pitiful piece of shit. They spoke to each other in their native tongue, and then they turned to leave.

"Noo! Don't go! Please!" I managed to scream, my throat burning and hoarse.

When I heard the heavy metal door slam, the sobs overcame me, and once and for all I just wished I was dead. I started to hyperventilate because the small room made me feel claustrophobic. I rocked back and forth in agony. *There is no fucking way Mario will find me now,* I thought.

SCARED TO DEATH

I don't really know how many days I was locked up in that dirty, dungeon-like room because there were no windows for me to see whether the sun was coming up or going down. I had no clue when the days changed.

I had slept so much that I wasn't tired anymore and started going stir-crazy. When I noticed all of the little bugs living in the room with me, I almost lost it. There were huge water bugs, small roaches, and every type of spider crawling over me while I tried to sleep on that fucking mattress. I jumped up and started brushing them off of me, but there was really nowhere for me to run to. I didn't even have on shoes to squash them with.

Never had I lived in conditions like this where bugs even came into contact with my fucking skin. Even when there were no bugs near me, I continued to feel like shit was crawling on me. I just kept brushing off my skin and scratching it. I felt like a mental patient locked up in an insane asylum.

I had tried screaming several times, until my throat was raw, but no one came. The sound of my voice just kept bouncing off the walls in an echo-like manner. That told me that the room was probably soundproof, so I really had no hope of anyone hearing me. I started to think that I would've been better off being sold at the auctions. Once I started thinking like that, I knew I was delirious.

I was hungry as hell, and it felt like I had not eaten in weeks. After what seemed like eternity, as I was lying on that horrible, thin-ass mattress, I heard keys tinkling outside of the door.

I sat up when I heard the noises, feeling mixed emotions. On the one hand, I felt nervous that those henchmen were coming back to kill me once and for all, but on the other hand, I was feeling kind of happy to have finally somebody coming in there to see me at all. I needed some human contact, and I was hoping they would at least give me some bread and water to survive.

As the door to my cell swung open, I sat up even more erect. When they walked into the room, I saw the same two Asian thugs who had tortured me and put me in that room. I hugged my knees to my chest and began rocking; I just knew it was my time to die. I looked up at them helplessly. I wanted to say something, but the words wouldn't come.

Finally one of the men said, "You come on. Time to go."

I swallowed hard as they both grabbed my arms and hoisted me up off the floor. When they stood me up on my feet, my legs kind of buckled from being so weak from sitting and lying down for so long.

"Where am I going now? Where are you taking me?" I asked in a raspy voice. I had already screamed my voice away.

"You go now," the other Asian henchman said with an attitude.

I think he was kind of pissed that I had the nerve to question him. They led me out of the room and back down the long hallway. When we were finally up out of the dungeon, I was happy to see sunlight coming through the windows of the house. I didn't remember ever appreciating natural sunlight like that.

After we reached upstairs, they handed me over to the same two Asian women who always took care of bathing and dressing me for the auctions. I smiled at the one who'd tried to help me, but she didn't smile back. She ignored my gesture and kept the same serious look on her face. I guess she didn't smile because she was in front of the other mean bitch, the older Asian woman. They took me back to the same room where I always went to get ready. I stared at the bed and longed to just climb into it and get a decent night's sleep. But that was just a dream. I knew what I was there for.

The nice woman handed me something to eat. It wasn't much— just some Chinese tea and a bowl of bland noodles. I was so hungry, I bent over that bowl of noodles and devoured it like it was steak and lobster. I didn't even take a minute to breathe.

The nice woman watched me closely. We were alone after the head woman gave her instructions to get me "cleaned up and ready to work" and left.

I saw the lady staring at me and I could tell she was looking at the bruises on my body. I instantly felt self-conscious and a little embarrassed. I tried to cover the marks with my hands.

"It's okay," the woman said sadly. She really looked like she felt sorry for me.

The look on her face made me just break down into racking sobs. I was kind of mad at myself for showing weakness, but I couldn't help it.

"They tortured me with electric shocks. They beat me and slapped me. I have been used and sexually abused. I have been put through some sick stuff, and I just can't take it anymore," I cried, putting my face in my hands. I was at my fucking breaking point.

The woman stood behind me and started stroking my hair. She

started speaking to me quietly real close to my ears. "You are lucky to be alive," she told me. "Many women don't make it out of here alive, especially with what you did, getting caught on the camera with the phone call. They let you live for a reason." She kept stroking my hair.

"I don't even care if they kill me! They should've killed me!" I screamed out hysterically. I was shaking all over. "I want to die! I am never going to get out of here, and I'd rather die than let these men keep on using and abusing my body!" I continued through racking sobs. I meant it too. I really felt like I had nothing to live for. I continued crying.

The woman looked at me sympathetically and continued stroking my hair. "Shhhh," she said. "You don't want them to hear you crying and saying that you want to die. They will kill you and think nothing more of you."

"I don't really care anymore," I said, sobbing.

"You have to live, Yoshi. You have to survive for the others. You are probably the only one that can help all of them now," the woman said.

I looked at her with a confused look on my face. I didn't know what she meant.

"Yoshi, my sister was just like you. We came here from China for a better life. In China a man promised us if we come to America we could work and make money to help our poor family back in China. My sister and I were very excited, and we jumped at the chance. But the promises were false. My sister was very beautiful and smart. I was motivated and determined to make a better like for myself, but when we got here, we learned really fast what they really had in store for us. The second day we were here, we were forced to sell ourselves to men," she said, her voice cracking.

I was just staring at her, waiting for the rest of the story.

"They made me sell my body until they said I was too old, then they made me work here, getting the women ready for the auctions. One day my sister got so tired of the abuse and the sex that she stole a cell phone from one of the auction customers. That was a big mistake. She tried to call the police so they could come and find her, but she was caught on the phone by one of the bodyguards at the customer's house . . . "

I was hanging on her every word, trying to find out what happened to her sister. I needed to know more about her. "What is your name?" I asked her.

"I am Ling. My sister was Meong," Ling said sadly.

"Tell me what happened when they caught her with the phone, if it's not too hard for you."

"When the bodyguards caught my sister with the cell phone trying to call the police, the customer beat her badly. They did unnatural things to her sexually and abused her with all types of objects, like hangers and metal tools. Meong was brought back to this house, and I couldn't even recognize her face, it was so bruised and battered.

"The customer wanted a refund of his money, one hundred and fifty thousand dollars. He blamed my sister and demanded his money back. The boss here didn't want to lose one of his best customers because of my sister's actions, so he gave the customer back his money. The boss wasn't happy with Meong because she caused him to lose a lot of money. He told her he would make an example of her for the others girls, just in case they tried to do the same thing. So he gathered all of the girls in a room. He stood Meong in the front and she was naked."

Ling started crying real hard. I was crying too, her pain and sadness was getting to me.

"He beat my sister with bamboo sticks on her body. I could hear her bones cracking under her skin as they beat her and beat her. When she couldn't stand up anymore, they made her kneel down, and they beat her some more. Her body was bloody, and she screamed from the pain caused by the broken bones in her hands, arms, and ankles. After they got tired of beating her, the boss walked up behind her and shot her in the back of her head. I watched my sister's brains explode out of her face right there in front of me and twenty of the girls."

Though Ling was crying, I could tell she was very angry and wanted revenge for what had happened to Meong.

"I'm so sorry about your sister," I said in a low tone.

Ling started wiping her face quickly, like she didn't want me or anyone else to see her crying. She started looking around frantically. I figured out that she must've known they were watching us and didn't want them to see her crying.

"Yoshi, I gave you the cell phone because I wanted you to call the police and get away. I want to free the other girls, but most of all, I want the boss and all of his thugs to go to jail forever. I picked you because your English is so good. When Meong and I came here, we couldn't speak good English. I think my sister would be alive if she could have told the police where she was and explain to them what was happening to her, but her English wasn't good. I think it was taking her too long to explain to the police, so she got caught."

Ling led me into the bathroom and turned the water in the big Jacuzzi tub on full blast. All of a sudden she was acting like she had before whenever she just bathed me and got me ready for the auction.

I was confused at first about her change of attitude, but she gave me a look with her eyes, and then I kind of caught on to what she was doing. She had turned on the water so whoever those fucking bastards had watching us on camera would not hear us talking.

I had been wondering why she was brushing my hair and speaking so closely in my ears when she was telling me about her sister's misfortune. I quickly caught on and just started playing along with her.

Ling kept the water running as she spoke to me. "I want to help you try to get away again, Yoshi," she said. "I want you to get away, so you can help all of the girls and help me get revenge for Meong's murder. You are our only hope, Yoshi. Just remember to tell the police that I was forced to work here and that I am not one of them," Ling said.

I stood with my mouth wide open. I couldn't believe what this lady was saying to me. She was really hell-bent on revenge, if she wanted to risk helping me again. I was sure that she knew they were watching me with the eagle eye.

"How will you be able to help me again? They are watching me like a hawk, and you will get yourself killed," I told her. I was growing kind of excited inside as my mind immediately started racing with thoughts of making a run for it and getting to Mario.

Ling put her fingers up to her lips to shush my questions. Then she signaled me to get into the bathtub. Once again she was bathing me just like she had before. Ling was silent for a long while as she went through the motions. I took her cue and sat down into the water. I winced at the pain the hot water caused me because of the bruises and scratches on my skin. But the lavender-scented flowers in the water made me feel relaxed and eased my senses.

Ling whispered, "Yoshi, if I help you get away, promise you will come back with the police and free us. Promise you will not betray me."

"I promise. I swear that if you help me get away I will make sure all of these muthafuckas suffer," I said. I was dead-ass serious too. I appreciated the fact that Ling wanted to help me, and deep down inside I told myself that I would not let her down if I made it out alive.

After Ling finished bathing me, she brushed my hair back out of my face. She pulled out some Dermablend Concealer cream and went about rubbing it into my skin to cover up all of the marks and bruises I got from my abuse. She also did my makeup and laid out a beautiful purple-and-black Nicole Miller dress for me. Ling helped me get dressed, and as I put on my clothes and she acted as if she was helping me, she kept whispering in my ears. She continued telling me all about the plan to get away.

"I am giving you a pocketbook and inside is a stun gun. Do not put the bag down at any cost," Ling whispered.

My eyes grew wide. "Where did you get that from?" I asked.

"There was a new girl last night. She was not cooperative. She didn't want me to bathe her or get her dressed. So they came in to make her cooperate. But the girl was not listening, and she started fighting with all of them. She was not afraid. The girl was very young, and she didn't want to go to auction. No matter what they did, she continued to fight them. One of the men went to use the stun gun on her, but she kicked it out of his hands. They finally just hit her with the back of a gun and knocked her out cold. They were so mad at her for fighting and so busy carrying her limp body away, they didn't remember to go back and get the stun gun. When they carried the girl out of the room, I secretly bent down and got the stun gun. I slipped it into my pocket and hid it all night. Yoshi, it is our only hope. Mine, yours, and the other girls' are depending on this. Now I am giving the stun gun to you, but you have to follow my plan closely."

My heart was already racing, just thinking about the possibility of us getting caught. Not only would the boss kill me this time, but Ling would surely be tortured then murdered.

Ling turned me around toward the mirror as she continued to act like she was just trying to help me get dressed. I can't front—Those Asians did a great job with makeup and dressing us up in that house. They spared no expense on dresses and accessories. It was crazy that they barely wanted to feed us, but they would dress us up so nicely. I guess that was part of their moneymaking scheme.

Once again, I looked beautiful, but I didn't feel beautiful at all. My planned escape gave me new motivation to get all dressed up and go out to auction. I was excited to be going to the auction this time.

Once Ling had told me what she had in mind, I started getting myself mentally prepared to do the deed. A stun gun would fucking certainly work out, if I could use it properly and make a run for it.

Ling told me, "Use the stun gun as many times as you need to get away from whoever buys you at auction tonight. But don't get caught, or else you will be dead, Yoshi."

Ling didn't say much more to me after that. It was just understood that I knew what the hell I had to do.

We heard noises outside of the room door, and both of us were real nervous, but we hid it well.

"She ready to go?" the older Asian woman asked as she came back into the room.

Ling nodded.

"Let us go then," the older woman said to me.

Ling gave me a knowing glance, and she finally handed me the pocketbook with the stun gun inside. I squeezed the bag a little bit just to make sure it was in there. I also gave Ling a look that told her I was ready to do this.

Before we knew it, the older Asian lady was leading me out of the room with her nasty-ass attitude. The lady suddenly stopped walking and started looking around, like she was suspicious of something.

After a few minutes, she stopped and turned to me, her face in a scowl. She looked me over from head to toe and then nodded her approval to the men who had followed her into the room. I knew right then and there that she wasn't onto me.

It was time for me to go to auction once again. As the older lady and two of the Asian henchmen led me out of the house, I looked back at Ling, and she gave me a tiny smile. I smiled back, being careful not to let any of the men or the old Asian woman see me. That smile and our eyes meeting was our little signal that shit was about to happen. I was about to make sure that I pulled out all of the stops to keep my promise to Ling and to save myself and all of those girls in that house who were suffering at the hands of these sex traffickers.

The old, selfish Yoshi would've just promised to help Ling and the other girls, but once she got what she wanted, she wouldn't have looked back. She would've turned her back on Ling and just thought about herself.

But something inside of me had changed. I told myself that as soon as I was far enough away from the danger of getting caught, I would definitely notify the police and bring down these deviant predators. I also told myself that if I made it out of this in once piece, I would find Lamar Patterson and Bryce and make both of those bastards suffer for what they had done to me. The only thing I had to do now was make it through another auction and use that fucking stun gun to fight my way to freedom.

THE ESCAPE PLAN

When we left the house in cars, I noticed we went in a different direction than we had before. The cars didn't go toward the highway and into the city this time. We finally got to another place, but it looked like we were still in Long Island. This was going to be a different auction house. I immediately got nervous because when I was going over my escape plans in my head, I had anticipated being in Manhattan when I got away. Now, shit had changed, which meant I had to change my plans. My mind started racing with different scenarios about my escape. My thoughts were interrupted when some of the armed men made me and all of the women line up. It was time for us to be sold off.

As I stood in the middle of the stage for yet another human auction, I looked out into the crowd of millionaires there to pay top price for a sex slave. I hated all of them. Some of them were dressed up, some of them smoked cigars, and I could definitely see diamond cuff links and pinky rings shining from the crowd. The bastards had so much money, paying a hundred or two hundred thousand dollars for a night with a woman was nothing for them.

I listened as the auctioneer called out the bidding price for the next girl up.

"Misty, a near virgin . . . bidding starting at fifty thousand. Do I have anyone for fifty thousand? We have fifty thousand? Do I have anyone for sixty thousand? Hey, I have sixty thousand."

As he continued belting out the numbers, the men in the crowd were raising their paddles to bid, and the girl on sale was turning around and around to show off her goods. It was a demeaning and humiliating process. I was growing angrier inside by the minute as I watched the girl being sold like a piece of property.

I kept hearing Ling's voice in my head saying, *"Yoshi, wait to use the stun gun until you are being transported to the house of the customer who ends up buying you at the auction. Wait until the right time, like when you are with less bodyguards around. Try not to let them take you into the house, or you might not make it out."*

"Yoshi!" I heard a man scream out, and then I was pushed from the back.

I was so busy daydreaming about Ling's instructions, I didn't realize it was my time up on the auction block. I immediately snapped out of my trance and moved out of the line to show off my body for bidding.

"Here we have Yoshi, a beautiful mixed breed with exotic features. Bidding starting at seventy thousand. Do I have seventy thousand?" the auctioneer called out.

I continued turning around like I knew I was supposed to. Each time I turned a full circle, the number on the bidding went up. I kept seeing paddle after paddle going up to bid on me. I guess I was a hot commodity because I was different than most of the other girls there. The higher the bidding got, the more evil I felt inside. I was having all types of wicked and murderous thoughts. This is what these men had made me into. I was picturing myself doing all types of violent sick shit to all of them. If given a chance I would've tortured them all.

I let a wicked smile spread on my face. They probably thought I was excited about the auction, but I wasn't. These bastards were bidding on me so they could do sick, nasty, perverted shit to me, but they had no idea what the fuck I had in store for the unlucky winner.

The bidding for me finally capped at one hundred and seventy-five thousand dollars, the highest number for the entire night. When I heard how much I had been sold for, I couldn't believe it myself. I was led off the auction stage and turned over to a tall, baldheaded man with very pale skin and stark green eyes. I watched him turn over the money for me, and before I knew it, he was back at my side, ready to lead me to his car.

When he started talking, I immediately recognized that he had a Russian accent. He tried to make small talk, but I was very short with him. I didn't have time for that bullshit, knowing what men like him were all about. In my opinion, there was no need for us to act like we were dating or like I was there voluntarily when we both knew the deal.

"Yoshi, I think you're beautiful," he said.

I just nodded.

"My name is Ivan," he said, introducing himself as he placed his arm around my shoulder.

I stayed quiet. What the fuck did I care what his name was? I just wanted him to take his hands off me. Ivan offered me a cigarette as we continued to wait for the valet to bring up his car, and I refused his offer. I just stood there, my body language stiff and rigid. I held onto my pocketbook like it contained the crown jewels. I was getting nervous, thinking about my plan, since I knew I wasn't far from the house this time. I shifted my weight from one foot to the other, feeling a lot of anxiety.

"You okay?" Ivan asked me.

I guess he could tell I wasn't feeling the current situation. I scrunched up my face. *Are you fucking serious? No, I'm not fucking okay, you dumb bastard! You're about to try to abuse my body, and you asking if I'm okay?* I screamed inside of my head. But what came out of my mouth was much different. "I'm fine," I said calmly.

Finally, I watched as an all-black Cadillac Escalade pulled up in front of us. The windows were tinted so dark, I couldn't see shit inside.

"Here we go, Yoshi," Ivan said as he forcefully grabbed my arm to make sure I got into the SUV.

I expected to see a bunch of bodyguards like usual, but it was only Ivan in the backseat with me and the driver up front. That made me feel real confident that I could get away. I sat stiffly in the backseat of the SUV, and Ivan climbed in and sat real close to me. At first I wasn't sure I would be able to get into my purse for my secret weapon if he was that close to me, so I had to start thinking quickly about how I would get him to move up off me a little bit.

Just like the rest of those bastards, Ivan wasted no time groping my tits and pushing his hands up my dress.

I squirmed out of his grasp. There was no way I was taking this shit. "Wait, I need to get a mint so I can kiss you," I purred, lying through my damn teeth. I was trying real hard to sound sexy to turn him on.

Ivan continued feeling me up for another few minutes. I looked out of the window and saw that the SUV had made it out of the garage of the auction place and was speeding down the street.

"Ivan, please. I want to get a mint from my bag," I said again.

He finally let go of me for a minute, and I slid a little ways from him and kind of turned my body sideways. I opened the pocketbook and dug down into the bag. My secret weapon was right there, just like Ling had told me.

I wrapped my hands around the stun gun just as the vehicle came to a stop at a light. I knew this was my fucking chance. My heart was racing like crazy as I turned with the speed of light and pressed that fucking stun gun up against Ivan's neck and pressed the surge button.

"Aghh!" he let out a pained sound, and his eyes popped open. That muthafucka's body started bucking, and he all of sudden went limp.

The driver looked up into the rearview mirror just in time to see me coming over the seat at him. Just as he was about to start moving the vehicle, I bent over the seat and stunned his ass too. But when I did that, his foot mashed down onto the gas, and the car sped out of control.

I lurched my body forward and grabbed the wheel to make sure we didn't go barreling into any trees or poles. That SUV was swerving all over the place, and I just knew I was about to die, but I was able to steer it away from a huge tree and onto a patch of grass.

I was finally able to come over the seat and get the vehicle under control. I stopped the shit on the side of the road and pushed that fucking driver right out onto the street. I stunned his ass again just to make sure he stayed knocked out. Then I opened the back door and struggled to drag Ivan's body, which felt like deadweight, out of the vehicle. I stunned him again too, just to make sure he didn't wake.

After struggling for a minute, I was able to get his big-ass body out of the truck. I reached into Ivan's and his driver's pockets and took their wallets, cell phones, and any cash they had on them. I also took the driver's gun out of his waistband. Then I hopped back into the driver's seat of the Escalade and peeled the fuck out of there.

"Oh my God! Oh my God!" I screamed out in joy as I raced the vehicle down the street. My fucking hands were trembling so badly, I could barely keep them on the steering wheel. I was so excited inside. Ling's plan had worked.

At first I didn't know if I should stop or keep going, because I didn't know who could have seen me dragging those bodies out onto the road. If anybody had seen me, they would surely have thought that Ivan and his driver were dead as doornails, the way I put their asses out there.

I stepped on the gas and kept checking the mirrors for any cops or any followers. I started recognizing some of the streets I was on and realized it was the way I had been driven so many times from the house to different auction places. I kept following that one road, but I was growing very anxious to find a spot to stop and call Mario and let him know I had gotten away. I was going to need his help for sure. There was no way I was going to let Ling down and not help her and the other girls at the house. Explaining this to Mario was going to be difficult, since I knew he would want me to just keep on running as far away as I could get until he could come and get me, but I was prepared to do whatever it took to get the police to the house to shut shit down over there.

After driving the Escalade for a few minutes, I decided to stop in a little alleyway not too far from the house to call Mario. As I dialed his number, my heart was beating fast. I don't know why I didn't just call the police first, like Ling had told me to do. I guess I was just pressed to speak to my man and let him know I was still alive. Shit, the last time he had spoken to me was when those goons had snatched me out of that room and I had to hang up on him. I knew he must have been sick to death with worry after that little episode.

When I was finished dialing his number, I put the phone up to my ear and noticed that my hands were still trembling. The phone started ringing on the other end of the receiver, and I was praying silently that he picked up. After the third ring, I started getting very nervous that he might not answer.

"C'mon, Mario, c'mon . . . pick up the fuckin' phone," I said out loud, like he could hear me. Just as I thought I would hear his voice mail, I heard his deep voice come through the receiver.

"Hello," he answered.

My shoulders slumped down with relief, and for a few seconds, I was at a loss for words, still feeling like my escape was all a dream.

"Hello?" Mario screamed into the phone.

I knew he was doing this because he didn't recognize the number. I finally screamed into the receiver in desperation, "Mario! It's me, baby! It's Yoshi, and I need your help!"

GET-BACK TIME

"Yoshi! Where the hell are you?" Mario screamed out.

I could hear both the excitement and concern in his words. He had probably been waiting by the phone for me to call him again. "I need you, Mario," I said. I was crying again so hard, I was out of breath.

"I know you need me, baby, but I need to know what the hell is going on and where the hell you're at. The last time we spoke—"

I quickly cut him off. We didn't have time for all of this small talk about what happened last time. We needed to deal with this present situation and the fact that I had escaped and needed to get away. "Mario, I escaped from them, and now I'm just stuck out here in Long Island. I have this truck that I stole and I don't know what my next—"

"So get the fuck out of there, Yoshi! Just keep driving and driving until you can't go no more. Get as far away from there as possible, and in the meantime, you can keep me posted on your whereabouts, and I'm going to work on my end to come and find you," Mario said all in one breath.

"You don't understand. I have to go back to that awful house. I can't just leave like this. I made a promise and I can't break it, Mario,"

I cried. I was so torn between running far away and keeping my promise to Ling. I know to him I sounded crazy, but it wasn't crazy to me. I had promised Ling that if she risked her own life and helped me escape, I would get the police back there and save all of the girls being sold. I couldn't break the promise. As bad as I wanted to just go, I couldn't bear doing that to Ling after all she had done for me.

"Go back to the house? What do you mean? A promise? To who? What the fuck are you talking about, Yoshi?"

"I know it sounds crazy, Mario, but there's a lady named Ling who works in that house of horrors and she helped me to escape. I promised her I would help the other girls get saved from those horrible men," I explained. I told Mario a quick version of the entire story about Ling, the first cell phone she had planted in my bag to help and about the stun gun she had given me this time.

Mario seemed like he understood what I was saying and why I wouldn't turn my back. But I know he was probably thinking, *Fuck that. Just get out of there.*

"Mario, I have to go back and get the address of that house so I can give it to the police so they can go there and save those girls. I have to go back. It is the least I can do for Ling."

"Yoshi, just wait. Let me do something first. This may be too dangerous for you to do alone," Mario told me. "Hang up the phone. I'll call you right back."

I thought he was crazy. "I don't have no time to wait for you to be calling me back!" I screamed. "Do you understand what I'm saying, that I am out here all alone and muthafuckas are probably looking for me right now?"

"Yoshi, just trust me please! Don't do anything stupid. I will call you right back. Your number came up on my cell phone caller ID screen, so I have the phone number to call you back. We have to be smart about this," Mario said and then he hung up.

I loved to hear him refer to us as "we." My heart melted for that man every time. So when he hung up, I did like he asked me and waited before I headed back over to the house to try to get the address.

Mario kept his word, and within ten minutes he called me back. This time he had that same FBI agent that I had spoken to before on the phone with him.

"Ms. Lomax?" the agent said into the phone.

"Yes. I'm here," I answered nervously.

"Are you all right?" he asked me.

I don't even know why he asked that stupid-ass question at a time like this. "No. I'm pretty fucked-up right now," I replied with an attitude. I wanted him to know his question was stupid to begin with.

"Okay. Well, Mario explained to me what's going on. The phone you're on is picking up on cell towers near Massapequa, Long Island. Do you see any signs saying that you're in Massapequa?" he asked.

"I don't see any signs. I am pulled over in an alleyway hiding out right now. Time is not on my side. I'm glad the cell towers told you where I am, but now what?"

"Ms. Lomax, you need to stay away from that house. You need to just get to a safe location, so we can send New York agents to pick you up and bring you to safety," he told me.

I wasn't trying to hear that bullshit. By the time they got their shit together, the boss might have found out that I had escaped and then shit would be bad for the girls and for Ling.

"Listen, I can't do that. You don't understand who these people are. Once they get word that I escaped, they will take all of those kidnapped girls and close up shop so fast, you and the whole fuckin' FBI will never find them. If that happens, the lady who helped me get away will be tortured and murdered for sure. They will make an example out of her, just like they did her sister. I can't let that happen. I promised her I would come back with the police and get her out of there."

"Ms. Lomax, what vehicle are you in right now?" he asked.

"I'm in an Escalade that one of the customers had picked me up in."

The agent asked me for more information, and I reached over to the glove compartment and retrieved the paperwork containing all of the information about the vehicle. I gave him the license plate numbers and read off the owner information from the registration—"Yelena Durkovic."

The agent sounded like he was writing down the information and calling it out to someone else in the background. I knew he was probably trying to get some agents to come find me in that vehicle, so they could try to stop me from going back to the house.

Once I figured out what he was trying to do, I put the car in drive and started driving in the direction of the house, determined to get that fucking address. I felt so stupid for not thinking of writing it down or taking a mental note of it before. Then again, with all the shit I had been through, going back and forth to that house, I gave myself a pass for not having the address.

"Ms. Lomax, I am just asking that you sit tight and let us do our job."

"I told you already. I can't do that," I said flatly. "You better just hurry up and send in some forces. Shit will get real bad, real fast if you don't. If you're really tracing this cell phone location, then you should be able to find me. I will keep the phone with me, so you can keep tracking me. If I get a chance to call you back with the address of the house, I will, if not, that means I'm in danger, and you need to send in the reinforcements as fast as possible."

"Yoshi, why don't you just fall back for a minute and let these men handle this situation? I don't want to risk losing you."

"Mario, I really do love you, but this is something I just have to do. I'm not the same anymore."

I had to explain to Mario that, after all I had been through since I had been abducted from the prison van, I wasn't the same selfish, self-centered Yoshi Lomax anymore. I really felt that I had to risk my own life to help the other girls and Ling. There were no if's, and's, or but's about it.

Mario finally gave in and told me he would work as fast as he could on his end to get someone to that house as soon as possible. All I had to do was keep that cell phone on me. I hung up with the hope that I would see him again very soon if all went according to plan.

I followed all of the landmarks I remembered passing, until I was up the street from the Long Island house where I had been bathed, tortured, and taken out for sale. My heart was beating really fast, and I was sweating because I was worried that some of the boss's henchmen might see me. Luckily, the windows on that fucking Escalade were tinted so dark, you couldn't see inside for shit.

I drove past the house gates slowly, so I wouldn't bring too much attention to myself. I just prayed real hard that as I passed the gates to get the address number they would never see me. Even though I drove by slowly, I could only see partially numbers of the address. I saw the guards eyeballing the Escalade suspiciously, so I knew I had to go around the block and stay back before they started to investigative further and realized it was me behind the wheel. Just being on the same street as that house made me fucking nervous.

I dialed Mario back and told him the name of the street and the partial number of the house. All I could do right then was hope for the FBI to piece together the clues to the house number and get there as soon as possible.

I sat in the vehicle and watched as girl after girl was paraded in and out of the house. "Better have your fuckin' fun now, you bastards, because you won't be doing this shit for much longer," I mumbled. It was time for me to get back at these bastards, and I couldn't wait.

Suddenly the cell phone rang. I looked down at it and saw Mario's number. I picked up the line.

"Yoshi, I think you should get the fuck out of there right now and not wait for the FBI or the police," he whispered.

"Why, Mario? Is there something I need to know?" I asked him.

"I just don't think you should trust everybody. Listen," Mario whispered again. "I gotta go. They're coming back in the room."

At first it took me a minute to catch on to what he was trying to tell me. But then it was like a lightbulb went off in my head. "Oh shit!" I said out loud to myself. *What if the FBI didn't believe me about the murder of those marshals? What if they were having me wait on them just so they could arrest my ass and extradite me right back to Miami?*

My thoughts were put on the back burner when I saw Ivan and his driver being helped out of a black Lincoln Town Car in front of the house.

"Oh my God!" I exclaimed. I couldn't fathom how they'd gotten to the house. "Somebody must've found them and helped them," I whispered to myself. They looked like they were still kind of dazed, the way they were walking with a little stagger. I was shaking my head back and forth, not believing my fucking luck. Now my heart was beating like a drum. The boss would know that I'd escaped. It wouldn't be long before he would be on a mission to find me, and on an even bigger mission to figure out just how the fuck I had gotten away.

I started thinking about Ling. I knew that once Ivan and his driver told the boss about the stun gun, it wouldn't take them long to figure out who was in that room the day the stun gun was dropped. All fingers would point back to Ling, and she would surely be killed. I could just imagine them pulling her down to the boss's office and beating her, torturing her, and then executing her in front of all the girls and other handlers to make an example out of her. Ling was on my mind like crazy.

But I also had other problems on my hands. The fucking FBI might've been trying to set me up for the downfall. As I sat there contemplating my next move, I saw three black cars with dark-tinted windows come barreling out of the gates of the house. I knew right away they were getting the boss out of there, since they figured the police would probably be coming soon. I also thought that Ivan and his driver might probably in one of those cars too, riding around with some of the boss's henchmen, trying to find me. All they had to do was spot the fucking Escalade, and I would be done. I was sure they weren't going to spare my life.

The damn FBI had not gotten there yet. I started to believe that my theory about them betraying me might just be valid. I mean, if they were really interested in bringing down this human trafficking ring, they would've been there already.

After I saw the cars leaving the house, something crazy snapped inside of me. I went into superhero mode. I just said to myself, since the FBI and the cops hadn't shown up yet, I was taking shit into my own hands. I wasn't about to let an opportunity for revenge slip through my fingers. No matter how dangerous the mission was, I was hell-bent on bringing the boss down and getting revenge for all of the abuse I'd suffered. I couldn't just let them all get away like that. So, out of nowhere and without thinking, I did the craziest shit I had ever done in my life.

CALCULATED DECISIONS

I cranked up the engine of the Escalade and started trailing behind the last sedan that pulled out of the house. I couldn't stand to lose them after all of the risks I had already taken. Deep down inside, I was feeling like, *What do I have to lose now?* I looked over at the gun I had taken from Ivan's driver and took comfort that I had it. I wasn't afraid to use it either, since every law enforcement agency in the country had already pegged me as a murderer anyway.

I followed the cars, making sure I stayed a safe distance back. Shortly after they left the premises of the house, something strange happened after that—One of the cars went east on the Southern State Parkway, and the other two took the ramp to go west. I had to make a quick, calculated decision, and so I followed the last two cars because something inside of me told me that the boss was in one of those last two cars. They drove for a while, and I stayed right on their ass, but far back enough that they couldn't see me. A few times I really had to maneuver the Escalade to keep up with them as they weaved in and out of traffic. It was crazy. As I followed them, my nerves were frazzled as hell.

Finally they exited the highway. Shit got tricky after that. I really had to keep letting other cars get in front of me, to keep my cover.

A few times I almost lost them, trying to be inconspicuous. The two black cars drove down what appeared to be a private road. I had to actually stop and let them go forward before I pulled back out. The little private road led up to another house. This house wasn't as big as the others, but it was just as nice, from what I could see of the outside.

I waited until they pulled onto the property before I drove up close enough to see if the boss was really there. I pulled over and stayed out of sight for a few minutes. The two cars stopped, and I saw a bunch of men getting out, but I still hadn't seen the boss.

I finally saw him get out and head into the house. I slammed my hands on the steering wheel, because I had the FBI on the way to the other fucking house.

Just then, three black vans whizzed past me on the private road and pulled into the property. What I saw next made me sick to my stomach. When the doors to the vans were opened, lines and lines of girls were herded out all chained together, so there was no way they could get out of there. They looked like animals being led to slaughter. Some of them were staggering from the drugs they had probably been given, and the sober ones were being pushed to keep them on their feet. I was so fucking mad, I bit down on my lip until I drew blood. The boss had brought all of the girls to this secret spot.

With my hands shaking, I immediately dialed Mario's number back. I needed him to get in touch immediately with that FBI agent to tell him what was going on. I needed them to hurry the fuck up.

"Hello!" I huffed into the phone, my anger coming across in my words for sure.

"Yoshi! What the fuck is going on? Where are you?"

"I had to leave from in front of the other house because the boss was trying to get away. The guy I escaped from came to the house, and I'm sure he told the boss I was gone."

As I was explaining the situation to Mario, I saw two more vans pull into the new spot. I looked on with my eyes wide as even more girls were offloaded from the vans. My suspicions were correct— The boss had moved all the girls to the new location. I could only imagine what would happen to them if I didn't stay there and wait for the police and the FBI.

"Yoshi, I'm glad you left the other spot, but you have to run now!" he screamed into the phone. "Get as far away from there as possible. It's all a setup. They're not on your side!"

"What are you talking about, Mario?" I asked in shock. I was gripping the phone, waiting for the words I didn't really want to hear.

"Yoshi, I overheard the FBI guys talking, and my suspicions were right—They don't believe your story about being kidnapped by that guy, and they think you had something to do with the murder of those marshals. They think you planned your escape along with Lamar Patterson so that you wouldn't have to face your trial in Miami. The FBI is acting like they want to help you save those girls, but really, all they want to do is capture you and bring you in."

Mario's words hit me like a ton of bricks, and my stomach immediately began cramping up. "These crooked-ass feds can't get shit right. I told them the truth, Mario. I didn't have anything to do with a fuckin' escape plan or the murder of those marshals. I was a victim here, and now I am risking my life to try to save these girls. I don't know who to trust anymore, Mario." I started crying into the phone.

"Listen to me carefully, Yoshi. I'm telling you to get the fuck out of there. I overheard the FBI agent I put you in contact with whispering on the phone, telling the New York FBI guys that they should track you down by the cell phone you are using and bring you in dead or alive. They also have you deemed as armed and very dangerous, so these agents are coming at you with big guns and no mercy."

I couldn't believe my ears. Here I was, waiting on the FBI to come save me and those girls, and they had other plans to fucking take me down or kill me in the process.

"Mario, I cannot believe these muthafuckas don't believe me!" I hollered. "Armed and dangerous? I am the least of their fuckin' problems right now, after all I have been through. Why would I stick around here if I was lying? Now I don't know what to do."

I was crying and shaking all over again. Even the good guys were after my ass. Once again, I was left with no plan as to what to do, and I couldn't even think straight. All I could think about was my promise to Ling. That was going to be a thing of the past now. Ling would think I betrayed her if I ran from there. But what choice did I have? I couldn't trust anyone but myself right then.

"Yoshi, I am suggesting that you drive and never look back. The way shit looks, you will not only have to be sentenced for Maria's murder, but you will also be charged with the murders of the two U.S. Marshals. We will never get to be together ever again if you don't get out of there, Yoshi. They are trying to send you to prison for the rest of your life. You know how the feds are—They are only interested in solving their cases at any cost."

I could tell Mario was serious and sad when he thought about us never seeing each other again. I felt the same way. "Look, Mario, I have to go. I don't know what I'm going to do or how I'm going to get away. If I never see you again, just remember that I love you very much," I told him. I meant my words too. I was really feeling like I would die at the hands of either the boss and his men or the fucking FBI.

"Don't talk like that, Yoshi. We *will* see each other again, I promise. You just need to get the fuck out of there and trust no man. I love you too, Yoshi."

My heart just melted, hearing Mario say those three little words. I sat in that vehicle crying hysterically and sick to my stomach. Mario's words about the FBI charging me with first-degree murder kept playing over and over in my head.

I suddenly felt dizzy. I opened the door of the SUV, leaned out, and threw up. After I did that, I realized the FBI could still trace my whereabouts with the cell phone I had. They had told me that they were picking up a signal on the phone from the cell towers. I thought that was a good thing because I'd thought they were coming to save me.

Then I thought, *They probably had Mario's phone bugged and heard our entire conversation.* Another wave of panic came over me. I knew it wouldn't be long before they tried to come to my location. In fact, I knew how the feds worked, so I knew they were on their way. I had made up my mind. I was taking Mario's advice and getting the fuck out of there.

Thinking quickly, I threw the cell phone out the window in front of the house gates. They weren't going to find me from tracking that fucking phone, but I was hoping that when they arrived thinking that they were getting me, they would run up into the house, bring down that bastard boss, and still go in and save Ling and the other girls. Too bad I wasn't going to be around to see all of those bastards led out in handcuffs.

I reached over into the passenger seat and picked up the gun. I placed it in my lap just in case I needed it right away. Then I looked around to make sure nobody was watching me before pulling the SUV back on to that little private road and driving the fuck out of there. I planned on getting far, far away. Wherever I ended up, I planned to contact Mario and either say good-bye to him or have him come on the run with me.

WANTED DEAD OR ALIVE

As I got the fuck out of there, I was flying down that little road, trying to hurry up and get to the outlet that led to the highway. When I got almost halfway up the road toward the highway, I saw a bunch of black vehicles speeding down the opposite side of the street toward the house. I knew right away it was the FBI coming for me. The FBI vehicles had lights atop them but no sirens blaring. They were trying to make a sneak attack. They just didn't know that I'd spotted them before they spotted me. Those bastards. Little did they know, when they got to the house, they weren't going to find me there.

"Oh shit!" I said out loud as I watched them flying by me. It was like my worst nightmare, seeing all of that manpower they had sent for little ol' me. They really thought I was an armed and dangerous fugitive. I quickly swerved the Escalade off onto the side of the road. It didn't seem like they'd seen me, but I had to make sure.

It was about ten minutes later before I saw the last set of lights drive past. I was gripping the gun I had in my hand so fucking hard, my hand started to hurt. I wanted to wait a good amount of time before I pulled out of there, just in case.

I took a deep breath and decided to make a move. I sat up in the seat and looked around nervously. I didn't see any more cars on the road, so I pulled out of the bushes and started for the highway and toward my escape. As soon as I moved the vehicle, I drove for a few feet, and all of a sudden, a car flew out of the side of the bushes in front of me.

"Oh shit!" I screamed, slamming my feet the brakes. The tires started screeching, that is how short I had to stop. I just barely missed hitting the vehicle that had pulled in front of me. My chest was heaving in and out. All I could see was my life flash before my eyes if I'd slammed into that fucking car. My nerves were even more on edge now.

"You fuckin' dummy! What are you doing!" I screamed at the strange car that had pulled horizontally into the road, almost causing me to hit it. I was blocked, so I couldn't move.

"Get the fuck out of the way!" I screamed, but all of my windows were up, and I knew the person driving the car couldn't hear me.

I couldn't see inside the windows of the strange car. It didn't look like one of the FBI cars, nor did it look like one of the boss's vehicles that he usually rode in. I figured it was probably somebody who had gotten lost on that little road.

"Move!" I screamed, rolling the window down a little bit. I didn't want to call that much attention to myself, so I didn't blow my horn for fear that I would attract attention, with all of the FBI activity going on up the street at the boss's other house.

As I sat there waiting for this car to move, I suddenly noticed headlights approaching from behind me. "Oh fuck!" I screamed.

They were coming toward the Escalade full speed ahead, and I knew right way that they were going to slam into the back of the vehicle. I was being trapped in. These muthafuckas were ambushing me.

"Fuck this!" I screamed, and I mashed down on the SUV's accelerator so hard, I could feel the floor of the vehicle. The Escalade went barreling into the stopped car, and I just knew that the airbag would deploy on me.

But luckily it didn't.

The Escalade had pushed the car a few feet, but not before the other vehicle slammed into me from the back, jerking my body, and I hit my head on the back of the seat, leaving me dazed and in pain.

As I tried to get myself together, the next thing I heard was loud bangs and glass crashing all around me. "Oh my God!" I screamed. Bullets were flying at me from the front and the back from both cars.

Just as I lifted up my hand to return fire, *BAM!*

I was shot in my shoulder. I felt fire radiate through my entire body.

"Aggghhh!" I screamed out in severe pain.

More bullets started flying over my head, and I got down low. I could feel blood soaking through my clothes. I was starting to feel dizzy from the pain.

BAM!

Another one of the wild shots hit me some place else on my body. More fire lit through my veins.

"Help me!!!" I let out a blood curdling scream. I felt like a heart was beating in my shoulder. I was in severe pain. I was trapped—a car in front of me and one behind me.

I lifted my opposite hand and let off a few shots from the gun I had, but since I couldn't see, I doubt if I hit anybody. Finally, the shots stop raining down on me, and I didn't hear shit for a few minutes. I said a silent prayer and just as I did the driver side door to the Escalade flew open. I could see body silhouettes but the faces were blurry. The gunshot wounds I suffered were making me real dizzy. I must have been losing a lot of blood. Still, I managed to get a kick off, but it was all for nothing. I was snatched out of the vehicle. My body was way too weak to fight.

"Get her into the other car."

I knew right away it was the voice of the boss. I wouldn't mistake his voice anywhere. He had climbed out of the car that had stopped in front of me.

I was in shock. "I thought . . . I thought you were at the house. I didn't see you leave again," I rasped out, barely able to get the words out of my mouth.

He contorted his evil face into a wicked smile. "Yoshi, you are not smarter than me," he said. "I can never let you know my moves. You brought trouble to me. You have to be taken out."

"You might as well. You and a whole bunch of people are after me," I said weakly, and my head drooped to the side.

"Let's get her out of here. I have to get far away from this place," he said to his men.

There was another car way up in front waiting for us. I was forced into the backseat and handcuffed.

"I need a doctor, or else I will bleed to death," I said.

"Well, if you bleed to death, it was all your own fault," the boss said to me.

Just as the car started to pull out, they started speaking in their language rapidly.

"Go, go, hurry up!" the boss screamed out in English.

I couldn't figure out what the panic was all about at first. Then I heard a loud noise outside. It was the sound of helicopters hovering over the area. Then I heard the distant sound of sirens wailing too. I knew then that the fucking FBI had finally caught on that I wasn't at the house and that the boss wasn't there either. I knew they weren't coming to save me either. They too wanted to take me down.

The loud sounds of the sirens made everyone in the car turn around and look out the back windshield. The blue and red lights were flashing rapidly. And at that point the police cars started gaining on the car I was in. They were all panicking.

The boss's henchmen started shooting at the cop cars.

"Oh shit!" I screamed out.

Once again, bullets were flying everywhere.

The helicopter overhead was now shining a bright light on the vehicle we were in. Those fucking Asians thought for sure that the FBI was there to take down their sex trafficking ring, but I knew better. They had never anticipated that one of their kidnapped girls was a fugitive from the law.

More bullets were flying, and all of a sudden the henchman in the passenger seat got hit in the head. His body slumped over, and the driver started swerving because the other guy's body almost fell into his lap.

"Drive! Drive!" the boss screamed as he held a gun to the driver's head.

I didn't care either way. It was a lose-lose situation for me. Either the Asians were going to kill me, or the fucking FBI would kill me or take me to jail for life for crimes that I didn't commit.

As we kept driving, I could tell there was more than one helicopter in the sky trailing the car. The helicopter got real low toward the highway. It was so low, I could see it from inside the car. That was the first time I had seen something like that, but I also remembered Maria telling me that the feds sometimes used snipers in helicopters to take down fleeing drug dealers. I had a feeling this was one of those instances.

Just as the thought entered my mind, I heard a loud bang. Then the windshield shattered, and the driver of the car slumped over. Blood splattered all the way into the backseat and got on me and the boss. The car was out of control and I just knew we would die.

"Aggghhhh!!!" I managed to scream out.

The boss put his gun to my head. He was about to shoot me, but he wasn't fast enough. Suddenly another shot whistled through the vehicle, and his head just exploded onto my face and body.

"Aggghhh!" I screamed out again.

The vehicle all of a sudden slowed down. The FBI had thrown out a rumble strip on the highway that punctured all of the tires on the car, stopping it instantly.

There was only one more muthafucka alive in that car with me. He pointed the gun at me and told me to get out of the car.

"I'm scared. They will shoot both of us," I said, trying to buy some time.

He wasn't trying to hear me. He grabbed me, and we exited the car together. He was using me as a human shield, holding the gun up to my head and screaming something in his language.

The FBI agents had surrounded the car, and there were guns drawn all over the place.

"Please! I'm not the criminal here! Please, believe me . . . I was kidnapped and forced," I started screaming.

The man holding me told me to shut up, with his broken accent.

"Release her, or you will die!" I heard some of the agents yelling.

I felt like I was dead already. He was choking the shit out of me, and he was crying. He knew that his life was over. He knew that this shit had all come to an end.

I also knew my fucking life was over because those FBI agents had fire in their eyes. As far as they were concerned, I had killed three federal law enforcement officers—Maria, and those two U.S. Marshals.

"I said let her go!" the agents yelled again.

But the Asian man just pressed the gun to my head even harder.

The next thing I heard was a bullet whistle past my head. I even felt the heat from it up against my face, and suddenly the man's arm was released from choking my neck, and his body collapsed on the floor.

That helicopter sniper was no joke. He had taken out the man holding me hostage without even harming me. At that point, I knew I had nowhere to run or hide.

I threw my hands up in surrender. My bullet wounds were killing me. I was ready to face whatever came next for me.

Those FBI agents descended on me like I was holding an arsenal of weapons. They wrestled me to the ground and roughly handcuffed me behind my back. I was screaming out in pain, but they didn't give a fuck about my injuries.

One of them started reading me my rights. I kept trying to plead my case.

Finally, I told one of the agents they needed to speak to Ling. I told them she would be able to tell them everything that happened to me. I'd shared my story with Ling. She'd also shared with me that she knew all about me, because the boss kept a record book in a safe. Ling said she had gotten to see the book one day while she was cleaning his office. He had forgotten to lock it back up.

Ling said the book kept a record of all of the girls, how they got to the house, where they came from, and how much money he made off them. When Ling had told me about it, I couldn't believe a big man in charge would be so stupid as to keep a written record of his crimes. But she told me it was true. I just needed to get to her now and find out where the book was.

III

I was taken to the hospital and my wounds were treated. I was locked down at the hospital and chained to the bed. There were a bunch of girls there from the house. The FBI was having them treated for injuries they had suffered. So all of my work wasn't all for nothing; at least the girls had been saved.

As I lay there thinking about how I was going to spend the rest of my life behind bars, I saw Ling walking by with one of the agents. Her face was badly bruised, and she was limping. My heart jumped. Ling had made it out alive.

I let a smile spread over my face. "Ling! Ling!" I called out.

She stopped walking and looked in my direction. "Yoshi?" she said, trying to see me through her black eyes.

"Yes, it's me!" I screamed.

Ling came rushing over to me. They couldn't stop her—she wasn't under arrest like me. The agent walking with her didn't look happy about our little reunion.

"Yoshi, thank you for keeping your word. I am sorry for what happened to you," Ling said. She was crying.

I knew that they had tortured her and was probably about to kill her, but the FBI had gotten to that house first.

"Ling, I need your help. Remember that book you told me about? I need you to find it. I need you to give it to my boyfriend Mario.

Don't give it to the FBI, because they will hide it and frame me. It is the only way they will believe my story," I whispered to her.

Ling nodded her head in agreement.

I whispered Mario's phone number to her, and she told me she was very good at memorizing numbers.

"Break up this little visit. Ms. Lomax is a prisoner. Let's go," one of the agents said to Ling.

I was glad I had enough time to give her the information she needed to help me. I knew she wouldn't let me down because she recognized that I had really risked my life to save her and the other girls.

Those bastard FBI agents took me from the hospital down to their cells in New York. They continued to try to question me about the murder of the marshals, but this time I was being smart. I wasn't speaking to them without first speaking to a lawyer. So they kept me sitting in jail for an entire week.

Finally, on one of the days I was sitting there, I heard footsteps coming toward the cells. I just figured they were coming back to harass me again, but when I looked up, I couldn't believe my eyes.

I had to actually rub my eyes because, after all I had been through, I just knew I was dreaming. Standing in front of me, dressed to death and looking sexy as hell, was my baby Mario. I threw my hands up to my face and just burst out in tears.

The guards opened the cell, and I jumped into Mario's arms. He held me so tight, I couldn't breathe. "How did you find me?" I said through my sobs.

"You have a real good friend, and she was looking out for you," Mario told me.

I knew right away he was talking about Ling. Then I noticed another man there with him.

"*Ahem! Ahem!*" the man cleared his throat like he was signaling to Mario that we had hugged and kissed enough.

"Oh, Yoshi, this is Mr. Schubert, you know, the lawyer I promised you before," Mario told me.

I couldn't stop crying from being so damn happy.

The man extended his hand to me for a handshake. When he did that, I noticed a book in his other hand. I could tell that it was the book that told the story. "How did you get that?" I asked softly.

"Your friend Ling gave it to us. I couldn't believe it when I read it. There are notes in here that corroborate your story. There are also notes in here telling that Lamar Patterson sold you into sex slavery and what country he fled to. The man running this criminal enterprise kept notes on everything. Strangely enough, he had dreams of one day selling his story to one of those gangster documentary shows," Mr. Schubert told me.

All I could do was smile. I was about to face the music, but the notes definitely sounded sweeter to my ears this time around.

My lawyer opened the book and turned to the page the boss had written about me. When he started to read, I was in shock. It was telling my story from the time I got sold. I knew between that book and Ling, I had an alibi that gave me a fighting chance to beat the added charges on me.

I reached out and grabbed Mario's hand. As long as he was by my side, I felt like I had nothing in the world to worry about.

EPILOGUE

The extradition back from New York was met with mixed feelings. Although I wanted to have my day in court to clear my name and resume my life and career, the thought of blowing trial was always lingering in the back of my mind. But I didn't want to leave Mario behind. He'd stayed with me through thick and thin, and I owed it to him to see it through.

The two stout U.S. Marshals were less than friendly. They both had that "cop" air, which meant their asses were stiff and mechanical like Arnold Schwarzenegger in *Terminator*. And they both wore Ray-Ban Aviator shades, one with a thin moustache, his counterpart, clean-shaven.

"Yoshi Lomax?" the marshal asked, as he read my name aloud from my transfer papers.

I nodded.

"Step back away from the bars and spread your feet apart and place your hands down by your sides."

His voice was authoritative, yet lacked inflection. He'd probably said those same words a hundred times a month. I can't even lie—I would never get used to having my hands and legs shackled like a damn wild animal.

I wobbled through the facility to the awaiting government van and took one last look at the New York skyline. I breathed in the polluted air and exhaled any lingering regrets. If I was going to beat the charges lodged against me, I couldn't do it without faith.

The ride from Metropolitan Detention Center to JFK Airport was roughly forty-five minutes. I read as we passed the large, colorful flight indicators—Delta. American Airlines. JetBlue. British Airways. Finally we parked in the cargo area, and I braced myself to be unloaded and transported through the airport. All I could think about was how embarrassing it was gonna be going through TSA and then to a domestic flight as a prisoner.

The guard removed my shackles from my arms and then stared at me intently. "Now why would you attempt yet another getaway?" he said.

"Excuse me?"

"Some people just don't learn when to throw in the towel," his partner said as he turned around in his seat to face me.

"I guess if you're attempting to get away, you'd need a gun, right?" He then pulled out a pistol and tossed it in my lap.

I sat there with my mouth hung open. *What's going on? Are they going to help me escape? Did Mario hire them to help me?* So many thoughts were going through my damn mind all at once. I couldn't speak. I reached down and picked up the pistol.

He shook his head. "Ahhh, man. You really shouldn't have done that. You should know better than to pull a gun on a federal officer."

Instantly I knew I was being set up for assassination.

I tried to take aim, but he was too quick. The first bullet hit my right shoulder, the second, my left.

I dropped the gun and yelped in pain. "Why are you doing this?" I cried out.

"Sheldon Chisolm sends his regards."

The next bullet lodged into my abdomen.

With my last ounce of strength, I lunged forward and tried to claw at his face. As the gun was rising up, all I could do was close my eyes and brace for impact. My head jerked once, and I felt the explosion.

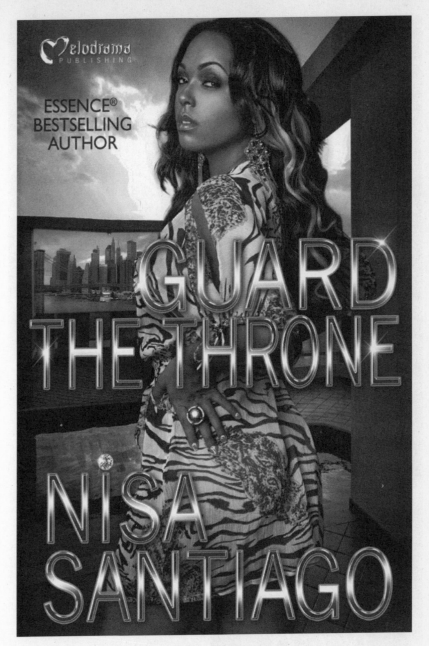

ESSENCE® BESTSELLING AUTHOR

GUARD THE THRONE

NISA SANTIAGO

Coming in October 2012

CONTROL IS THE GAME. MONEY IS THE PRIZE.

Follow
MELODRAMA PUBLISHING

www.twitter.com/Team_Melodrama

www.facebook.com/MelodramaPublishing

MELODRAMAPUBLISHING.COM

MELODRAMA PUBLISHING ORDER FORM

TITLE	ISBN	QTY	PRICE	TOTAL
10 CRACK COMMANDMENTS by ERICA HILTON	978-1-934157-21-3		$15.00	$
BAD APPLE: THE BADDEST CHICK (Pt 1) by NISA SANTIAGO	978-1-934157-45-9		$14.99	$
CARTIER CARTEL by NISA SANTIAGO	978-1-934157-18-3		$15.00	$
CARTIER CARTEL MM by NISA SANTIAGO	978-1-934157-34-3		$ 6.99	$
CHECKMATE: THE BADDEST CHICK (Pt 3) by NISA SANTIAGO	978-1-934157-51-0		$14.99	$
COCA KOLA: THE BADDEST CHICK (Pt 2) by NISA SANTIAGO	978-1-934157-48-0		$14.99	$
DEAL WITH DEATH by ENDY	978-1-934157-12-1		$15.00	$
DIRTY MONEY HONEY by ERICA HILTON, NISA SANTIGO, KIM K	978-1-934157-44-2		$14.99	$
DIRTY LITTLE ANGEL by ERICA HILTON	978-1-934157-19-0		$15.00	$
DRAMA WITH A CAPITAL D by DENISE COLEMAN	978-1-934157-32-9		$14.99	$
EVA II: FIRST LADY OF SIN MM by STORM	978-1-934157-35-0		$ 6.99	$
GUARD THE THRONE by NISA SANTIAGO	978-1-934157-50-3		$14.99	$
I'M STILL WIFEY (Pt 2) by KIKI SWINSON	978-0-9717021-5-8		$15.00	$
IN MY HOOD by ENDY	978-0-9717021-9-6		$15.00	$
IN MY HOOD MM by ENDY	978-1-93415757-2		$ 6.99	$
IN MY HOOD 3 by ENDY	978-193415762-6		$14.99	$
JEALOUSY: THE COMPLETE SAGA by LINDA BRICKHOUSE	978-1-934157-13-8		$15.00	$
JEALOUSY by LINDA BRICKHOUSE	978-1-934157-07-7		$15.00	$
LIFE AFTER WIFEY (Pt 3) by KIKI SWINSON	978-1-934157-04-6		$15.00	$
LIFE, LOVE & LONELINESS by CRYSTAL LACEY WINSLOW	978-0-9717021-0-3		$15.00	$
LIFE, LOVE & LONELINESS MM by CRYSTAL LACEY WINSLOW	978-1-934157-41-1		$ 6.99	$
MENACE by MARK ANTHONY, AL SAADIQ BANKS, J.M. BENJA-MIN, ERICK S. GRAY, & CRYSTAL LACEY WINSLOW	978-1-934157-16-9		$15.00	$
MURDER WAS THE CASE by KIKI SWINSON	978-1-934157-54-1		$14.99	$
MYRA by AMALEKA MCCALL	978-1-934157-20-6		$15.00	$
RETURN OF THE CARTIER CARTEL by NISA SANTIAGO	978-1-934157-30-5		$14.99	$
RISE OF AN AMERICAN GANGSTRESS BY KIM K.	978-1-934157-53-4		$14.99	$
SHEISTY CHICKS by KIM K.	978-1-934157-47-3		$14.99	$
SHOT GLASS DIVA by JACKI SIMMONS	978-1-934157-14-5		$15.00	$
A STICKY SITUATION by KIKI SWINSON	978-1-934157-09-1		$15.00	$
STILL WIFEY MATERIAL (Pt 4) by KIKI SWINSON	978-1-934157-10-7		$15.00	$
STRIPPED MM by JACKI SIMMONS	978-1-934157-40-4		$ 6.99	$
TALE OF A TRAIN WRECK LIFESTYLE by CRYSTAL LACEY WINSLOW	978-1-934157-15-2		$15.00	$
THE CRISS CROSS MM by CRYSTAL LACEY WINSLOW	978-1-934157-42-8		$ 6.99	$
THE DIAMOND SYNDICATE by ERICA HILTON	978-193415760-2		$14.99	$

CHECK CATALOGUE RELEASE DATES
BEFORE PLACING AN ORDER

MELODRAMA PUBLISHING ORDER FORM
(CONTINUED)

TITLE	ISBN	QTY	PRICE	TOTAL
WIFEY (PART 1) by KIKI SWINSON	978-0-9717021-3-4		$15.00	$
WIFEY 4 LIFE (PART 5) by KIKI SWINSON	978-1-93415761-9	.	$14.99	$
WIFEY 4 LIFE (PART 5) MM by KIKI SWINSON	978-1-934157-43-5		$6.99	$
WIFEY: FROM MISTRESS TO WIFEY by ERICA HILTON	978-1-934157-46-6		$14.99	$
WIFEY: I AM WIFEY (PART 2) by ERICA HILTON	978-1-934157-52-7		$14.99	$
YOU SHOWED ME by NAHISHA MCCOY	978-1-934157-33-6		$14.99	$

Instructions:

*NY residents please add $1.79 Tax per book.

**Shipping costs: $3.00 first book, any additional books please add $1.00 per book.

Incarcerated readers receive a 25% discount. Please pay $11.25 per trade paperback book and $5.25 per mass market (MM), and apply the same shipping terms as stated above.

Mail to:

MELODRAMA PUBLISHING : P.O. BOX 522 : BELLPORT, NY 11713

Please provide your shipping address and phone number:

Name:_____

Address: _____

Apt. No: _____ Inmate No: _____

City: _____ State: _____ Zip: _____

Phone: ( ) _____-_____

Allow 2 - 4 weeks for delivery

BULK ORDERS, CALL 347-246-6879 FOR DISCOUNTS.

WRITE ALTERNATE TITLE(S) IN CASE BOOK IS OUT OF STOCK.

_____

_____